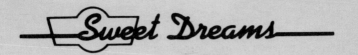

DREAMSKATE

Angela Cash

BANTAM BOOKS
NEW YORK • TORONTO • LONDON • SYDNEY • AUCKLAND

RL 6, age 11 and up

DREAMSKATE

A Bantam Book / February 1994

Sweet Dreams and its associated logo are registered trademarks of Bantam Books, a division of Bantam Doubleday Dell Publishing Group, Inc. Registered in U.S. Patent and Trademark Office and elsewhere.

Cover photo by Kim Hanson.

ISBN 0-553-56475-7

Published simultaneously in the United States and Canada

Bantam Books are published by Bantam Books, a division of Bantam Doubleday Dell Publishing Group, Inc. Its trademark, consisting of the words "Bantam Books" and the portrayal of a rooster, is Registered in U.S. Patent and Trademark Office and in other countries. Marca Registrada. Bantam Books, 1540 Broadway, New York, New York 10036.

PRINTED IN THE UNITED STATES OF AMERICA

OPM   0 9 8 7 6 5 4 3 2 1

DREAMSKATE

"Thanks for letting me take you home, Lindsey," Paul said softly.

For a brief moment I wondered what it would be like if he wrapped his arms around me and held me close. What would it be like if he kissed me, his soft, full lips pressing against my own . . . ?

Flustered, I bent down to pick up my bag, then reached for the door handle. "Thank *you* for driving me," I said. "It was really nice of you. And thanks for the hot chocolate too."

Paul smiled and leaned closer, so close, in fact, that I thought he actually *would* kiss me. I held my breath.

"Lindsey . . ." He hesitated, and I hoped he was going to say something thrilling. But all he said was "You're welcome."

I forced myself to open the door and got out of the car. "Good night," I murmured.

As I went inside my house, my feet hardly seemed to touch the ground. Even though it was crazy, I knew I was head over heels in love with Paul Taylor.

Bantam Sweet Dreams romances
Ask your bookseller for the books you have missed

DREAMSKATE

DREAMSKATE

Chapter One

"Hey, Lindsey, watch this!"

I glanced over at my best friend as she leapt into the air, then watched in dismay as she spun out of control, her arms and legs flailing wildly. "Oh, Karen, be careful! Watch out for the—"

Thump!

"Wall," I finished lamely, and quickly skated over to where she was sprawled on the ice. "Karen? Are you okay?"

She moaned slightly, and rubbed the back of her head. "Did I ever tell you how much I hate ice-skating?" She glared up at me, but her dark eyes were sparkling.

"Only about a thousand times! And it's no wonder, the way you skate. Really, Karen, you do the weirdest things!" I held my hand out to her and pulled her to her feet.

"Weird? You're calling my skating weird?" She scratched the tip of her nose with a red-gloved finger. "I'll have you know that what I just attempted was the famous Karen Anderson double-trouble loop-de-loop."

"Oh, you!" I shoved her playfully, accidentally causing her to lose her balance. Only this time when Karen fell, she grabbed hold of my sleeve and took me with her.

"Hey! Just what do you think you're doing?" I joked good-naturedly as we struggled to get up.

Karen laughed. "Oh, just teaching Miss I'm-Suzy-Skater-and-I-never-fall-down what it feels like to fall down!"

"Gee, thanks a lot!"

"No problem."

While we wiped the slush off our jeans, I glanced over at my friend. Her dark shoulder-length hair was thick and curly, and her big brown eyes were fringed with ridiculously long lashes.

"What's wrong? Why are you staring at me

like that?" Karen asked. "Do I have something gross hanging out of my nose or something?"

I laughed. "No. I was just thinking how pretty you are, and how I wish I had half your looks, and—"

"Lindsey!" Karen shrieked. "Knock it off! You have got to be kidding! You're much prettier than I am. Your eyes are such a gorgeous blue, and your hair—it's so . . ."

"Red?" I suggested sarcastically.

"No," sighed Karen. "You know, I love your hair—I've told you so only about a million times. I think they call that color titian."

"Well, that's just a fancy word for red. And you're crazy for liking it." I reached back to retie the bow that was holding my ponytail in place. Left loose, my hair hung just past my shoulders, but it was so unruly that I almost always pulled it back. "Besides," I added, "I'm too skinny and short. My brother calls me a shrimp."

"Since when did you start believing what Luke says? You're too hard on yourself," Karen said. "Just because you don't have a boyfriend at this particular moment in your life doesn't mean you're not pretty. Neither do I, and you don't hear me complaining, do you?"

3

I smiled. "Yeah, but you've had plenty of them in the past, and I've never had even one."

"But not because you couldn't." Karen gave me an impish grin. "You know, Trent Peterson really likes you."

"I know," I said glumly. "Don't remind me! He follows me around everywhere. It seems like I spend half the day trying to avoid him."

"Well, I think he's kind of cute."

Sighing, I said, "Karen, he's only a sophomore."

"So what?" she said. "But see, you *could* have a boyfriend if you really wanted one."

I shook my head and laughed. "Okay, okay. You made your point. C'mon, let's skate some more." I started to glide forward, but Karen yanked my arm so hard, I almost fell.

"Oh, Lindsey, look! Who is *that*? He's incredible!"

I looked at the other skaters on the ice. "Who? I don't see—"

Then suddenly I did. A slender yet muscular boy was in the middle of the rink, expertly going through numerous spins and twirls. He hadn't been there a moment earlier, and I was sure I'd never seen him at the rink before.

Still, something about him seemed very familiar. I just couldn't put my finger on it.

"Isn't he gorgeous?" Karen breathed.

I nodded. "Yeah."

The boy had dark chestnut-colored hair
that waved softly around his face. He was tall,
maybe six feet, but from where we were
standing it was hard to tell exactly.

"Just look at him, the way he moves. It's so
beautiful," Karen sighed.

Silently, I agreed. We watched in awe as he
executed several difficult jumps, spinning and
landing effortlessly on the ice. Several other
skaters had backed up against the sides of
the rink, watching this new skater as intently
as I was.

"It's like he's someone special, you know?"
Karen added softly. "Like the skaters in the
Olympics."

And that's when I knew why he seemed
so familiar. "That's it! Karen, that's it!" I
exclaimed.

"What? What's it?"

"Him!" I whispered. "It's *him*!"

"Who?"

"Karen, that's *Paul Taylor*!"

Karen stared at me blankly. "Who?"

5

"Paul Taylor! Karen, he was in the Olympics. That's where I've seen him before!"

"Really?" Karen's eyebrows shot up. "Did he win a medal?"

I shook my head. "No, but I think he just barely missed getting the bronze. I remember watching him on TV. I taped all the figure skating coverage, you know."

Karen nodded. "But are you *sure* that's him?"

"Yes!" I said excitedly. "I can't believe I didn't recognize him sooner. I mean, I've watched those tapes over and over. I guess I just never focused on him that closely."

"Well, he's certainly worth focusing on." Karen grinned. "Too bad there aren't any guys like him at Pine Ridge High. I wonder what he's doing here?"

"I don't know. I mean, Pine Ridge Skate Club is the last place I'd expect to see a skater like Paul Taylor. This certainly isn't the best place to practice for championship events. Unless . . ."

"Unless what?"

"Well," I continued, "unless he's not skating in competition anymore. Maybe he's turned pro."

6

"Yeah, but that wouldn't explain why he's skating here in Pine Ridge."

"True," I admitted.

"Well, whatever the reason, I just may have to start spending a lot more time at the rink!" Karen said, giggling.

"But you hate skating," I reminded her.

"All of a sudden I'm liking it a whole lot more!"

We both laughed, and I continued to watch Paul Taylor with admiration. How I wished I could skate with the self-assurance he possessed! And that's when I realized I wouldn't be satisfied until I could talk to him. Somehow, some way, I was determined to meet Paul Taylor.

The next morning I plopped down on a chair at the kitchen table and stacked my books and homework next to me.

Dad smiled at me over his paper as I reached for the box of granola.

"Tuna fish or peanut butter, Lindsey?" Mom asked as she raced around the kitchen, throwing together brown-bag lunches for my brother and me.

"Tuna fish, please."

7

"Don't fix me anything, Mom. I'm having school lunch today." My older brother, Luke, slid into his seat across from me and hurriedly began fixing himself a bowl of cereal. "Anything new on the sports page?" he asked Dad.

Dad flipped through the newspaper until he found the sports section. "Well, there's an article here about a former Olympic skater who's now attending Pine Ridge High. His name's Paul Taylor. You kids seen him yet?"

I actually dropped my spoon, splashing droplets of milk all over the table.

"Yeah," Luke replied. "I've got a couple of classes with him."

"You know Paul Taylor? *The* Paul Taylor from the Olympics?" I gasped.

Luke nodded. "Yeah. Well, I don't really *know* him, but I know who he is."

I struggled to control my voice. "You mean to tell me that Paul Taylor goes to our very own school and you never even mentioned it until now?"

Luke stared at me. "Chill out, Lindsey. He's only been here since Monday. Besides, what's it to you?"

I shrugged, trying to regain my composure. "Nothing. It's just that—well, you know how I

8

feel about skating and the Olympics, and . . ." My voice trailed off.

"Hey, you have a crush on Paul Taylor, right?" Luke grinned broadly.

"No," I answered quickly. "Of course not. That's so stupid! I didn't even know he went to our school until just now. How could I have a crush on someone I've never even met? Get real." But I felt my face grow hot anyway and knew that two bright-red splotches were appearing on my cheeks.

"You do too!" Luke crowed. "I can't believe it! My little sister has a crush on a big Olympic athlete!"

"Luke!" I glared at him over the table. "I do not!"

"Then why is your face turning all red? You look like a giant tomato."

"Luke," Mom said sternly, "eat your breakfast and stop tormenting your sister."

My eyes shot daggers at him while we finished our breakfast, but Luke just grinned at me, knowing he was right. What made it worse was knowing that *he* knew that *I* knew he was right.

A few minutes later Luke glanced at his watch and pushed back his chair. "I've got to get going. You better move it too, Lindsey," he added as he left the kitchen.

Just then I heard the familiar honking of Karen's Volkswagen horn.

"That's my ride." I stood up and took a final gulp of my orange juice, peering over my father's shoulder at the paper.

"Dad?"

"Hmmm?"

"Are you by any chance done with the sports page yet?"

He turned back a few pages and handed me the section. "Here you go."

"Thanks!" I grabbed my lunch and my books, struggled into my coat, and dashed out the front door.

"Oh, Karen, you'll never guess what I have!" I sang out as I got into the car.

"Good morning to you too!" she teased.

I waved the sports section excitedly in front of her. "Do you know what this is?"

Karen turned to look at me. "Is this a quiz?"

"Karen . . . !"

"Okay, okay. Let's see—is it a—could it possibly be—a *newspaper*?"

"Yes!" I said, ignoring her sarcasm. "But this isn't just any old newspaper!"

"I give up." Karen threw up her hands. "Just tell me what's so special about it before I die from the suspense."

Quickly, I flipped to the page with the article on Paul. "Guess who's attending Pine Ridge High?"

"Who?"

"Paul Taylor!"

"Paul Taylor? Olympic-skater Paul? As in Paul-at-the-ice-rink-yesterday?"

"Yes!"

"Are you kidding?"

"No! It's all right here! There's a whole article about him in the sports section of this morning's paper."

"Well, what does it say?" Karen asked as she pulled away from the curb.

"I don't know," I admitted. "I haven't had a chance to read it yet."

"Well, what are you waiting for? Read it now!"

I turned to the article and scanned it while we drove along. "Basically, it just says that he's gone pro and will be touring with the Professional Ice Skaters Team after he graduates." I held up the paper. "And look, there's even a picture of him!"

11

"Ohhh, he is *so* cute!" Karen exclaimed, glancing over at the photo. "But why is he going to school here? I mean, wouldn't it make more sense for him to be going to school in his own hometown, wherever that is?"

"Who knows? Maybe his family just moved here or something."

We arrived at school and headed toward the locker we shared. "Just think, Karen, Paul Taylor is in this very school at this very moment!" I sighed. "Can you believe it?"

"I'll believe it when I see it." She began dialing the combination to our locker. "Here, give me your stuff." She piled the books we didn't need right away onto the shelves. "What about that?" She motioned to the paper I still clutched in my hand.

"I'm going to take this with me," I told her. "I want to read it again."

Karen rolled her eyes. "Jeez, Lindsey, you've really fallen for this guy, haven't you?"

"Don't be silly! I have not!" I protested.

Karen just stared at me, a half-smile on her face. "You keep forgetting that we've been friends since fifth grade. I know you inside and out, Lindsey. Here, take your stuff."

I grabbed my French books from her as the

first bell rang. "See you later," I said, and headed off in the direction of Monsieur Roberge's room. As I made my way through the crowded hall, I tried to read the article for the second time. All of a sudden I ran into somebody and my books and papers went flying. Annoyed, I bent down to pick them up before they were trampled in the stampede.

"Hey, I'm really sorry. I guess I wasn't watching where I was going. Here, let me help you."

I looked up to see who the unfamiliar male voice belonged to, and when I did, I almost fainted.

"You're not hurt, are you?" Paul Taylor had crouched down to my level and was looking intently at me. His eyes were hazel, with little specks of green in them, and he had the most wonderfully long lashes I'd ever seen, even longer than Karen's.

I knelt there, gaping at him, unable to think of a single thing to say.

Paul picked up my belongings, and when he handed them back to me, his hand brushed against mine, sending shivers up my spine. "Here you go," he said. "I really am sorry . . ."

We both stood up then, and I noticed he was at least a foot taller than I was.

"No, *I'm* sorry. It was my fault . . ." I faltered, mesmerized by his gaze. "I guess trying to read and walk at the same time wasn't such a good idea."

"That'll do it to you every time!" Paul flashed a warm smile, and a dimple appeared in his left cheek. "Oh, wait, you forgot this." Quickly, he picked up the newspaper at his feet and glanced at it before giving it to me. "Sports nut, huh?"

I nodded, dying of embarrassment. If only he hadn't noticed that the paper was open to the article on him!

Chapter Two

"Now, tell me again. What were his exact words?" Karen demanded as she laced her left skate that evening.

"Karen," I sighed, "I already told you. I can't remember exactly."

"How can you not remember a conversation with Paul Taylor, your dream guy?"

I finished lacing up my own skates and sat up. "I don't know. I was in shock, I think. Those eyes, Karen! They were incredible. And his smile—he has a dimple! It's so cute!"

Karen groaned. "Good grief! Give this girl a cold shower before she melts on the spot!" I elbowed her playfully, and she laughed. "How did it all end?"

"Well . . ." I thought a moment, relishing every detail I could possibly remember. "After he handed me the newspaper, he started to leave."

"Then what?"

"Oh," I said, "then he turned around and told me his name. As if I didn't already know!"

"And did you tell him yours?"

I wrinkled my forehead, trying to remember. "I don't think I said anything. I just stood there like an idiot."

"At least you're a *cute* idiot," Karen teased. "Say, you owe me big time for coming to skate with you tonight. We were supposed to go to the mall, remember?"

I held up my right hand. "I solemnly swear we'll go this weekend. I just need your support tonight."

"Well, okay. But if Paul doesn't show up, I'm *not* coming back again tomorrow, understand?"

I nodded and scanned the rink. It was seven-thirty, peak time for recreational skaters, but the evening seemed rather quiet, and there was no sign of Paul. After literally run-

16

ning into him that morning, I could think of nothing else but seeing him again. And since we had no classes together and didn't even share the same lunch period, I figured the only way I was ever going to see him again was on the ice. So I planned on spending as much time as possible at the rink.

Karen and I skated for half an hour before taking a break.

"I guess he's not going to show up," Karen stated matter-of-factly.

"He's just *got* to!"

"Okay," she said. "Let's suppose he does. Then what are you going to do? Are you going to talk to him, or what?"

I shrugged. "I don't know. I haven't thought that far ahead yet."

"You are absolutely hopeless, Lindsey! You've got to have some sort of a plan."

"Like what?"

"Well . . ." Karen frowned. "Let me think about it. I'll come up with something."

We started skating again, and I practiced a couple of my combination jumps. I was feeling pretty good about landing all the jumps I'd tried, so I gathered up some speed and attempted a double axel. It was a jump that had taken me months to learn, and more often than not I still couldn't land it. Normally I wouldn't have tried such a difficult jump in public, but for some reason I was feeling as if I could do just about anything. And I did it! It was probably the best double axel I'd ever done. I could hear Karen cheering as I hit the ice square and hard.

"All right!" she shouted, and let out a piercing whistle.

I threw back my head and laughed. As I glided to a stop, Karen pulled up beside me. "That was a great jump, Lin! I was really impressed, and I bet Paul was too." She smiled mischievously at me.

"What?" I gasped.

"Look." Karen nodded behind me and I slowly turned my head. There, standing at the rink's entrance, was Paul Taylor.

I immediately turned back to Karen. "Why didn't you tell me? I can't believe this! How long has he been there?"

She shrugged. "I don't know, honest! I spotted him right before you did that axel thing—"

"Double axel," I said automatically.

"Whatever. Anyway, by then it was too late

to warn you. I suppose I could have shouted across the ice that he was here, but somehow I didn't think you'd appreciate that."

"Good thinking." I tried to remain calm. "What's he doing now?" When Karen looked over my shoulder, I said, "Don't be so obvious!"

"Would you just relax?" She turned back toward me. "Do you really want to know?"

"Yes!"

"Well, at this particular moment he's staring at you."

"No way!" I gasped.

"Lindsey, I'm not kidding."

I took a deep breath. "Okay, what's the plan?"

"Plan? What plan?"

I gritted my teeth. "The one you said you were going to think up for me."

"Oh, *that* plan . . ."

"Well?" I said impatiently. "What is it? Are you going to tell me or not?"

I was trying very hard to stay cool. On the one hand, I was glad that Paul had witnessed my spectacular jump, but at the same time I also fervently hoped he didn't think I had done it just to impress him. The last thing I needed was for Paul Taylor to think I was a show-off.

"Well . . ." Karen finally answered, "I don't think we're going to need a plan."

"Why not?"

"Because he's skating right toward us."

"You're kidding, right?" I squeaked.

"Nope. Here he comes."

"Karen! What am I supposed to do?"

She only grinned at me. "Get ready, get set . . ."

"Hi."

I spun around and found myself staring up into those wonderful hazel eyes again. "Hi," I mumbled, and began to blush.

For a minute nobody said anything. I wished I could disappear. Why was I always at such a loss for words when it came to speaking to members of the opposite sex, particularly gorgeous ones?

"That was a great double axel." Paul smiled, and his dimple reappeared.

"Thanks." *Oh, real clever, Lindsey,* I thought.

"Do you take lessons?"

I shook my head. "Not right now. I used to though."

20

"She teaches herself a lot of jumps and stuff from books," Karen volunteered, grinning widely. "She practically eats, sleeps, and lives skating."

I wanted to kick her, tell her to shut up or something. She was really embarrassing me.

"Well," Paul said, "you're pretty good. You ought to consider taking some more lessons. With a little work I think you could be an excellent skater." He stressed the word *excellent*, and I felt my cheeks burning. "By the way," he added, "you never did tell me your name this morning."

"It's Lindsey Matthews," Karen told him when I didn't say anything. "And I'm Karen Anderson."

"Nice to meet you both." Paul smiled at us. "I just started school here this week and I don't really know many people yet, especially people who like to skate."

"Well, you and Lindsey should get along real well," Karen said. "Like I said before, she lives to skate. She even taped all the ice-skating coverage from the last winter Olympics. She watches it all the time."

"Karen . . ." I said in a threatening tone, hoping she'd get the hint and stop babbling.

21

"Oh, wow!" Paul groaned. "I sure hope you don't watch *my* performance very often—it definitely wasn't my best."

"Oh, I thought it was fantastic!" I said breathlessly. "Your free style was excellent, and your compulsories weren't bad either. I bet you would have won the bronze if you'd landed a couple of your jumps more solidly."

Paul raised his eyebrows. "Really?"

I wanted to drop right through the ice. I couldn't believe that I had just criticized Paul's performance in the Olympics! Who was I to tell him how he had skated or what mistakes he'd made? He'd probably never speak to me again.

Then he smiled. "You know, that's exactly what my coach said too. You really *do* know skating."

I smiled too, weak with relief.

"Well," Karen said cheerfully, "I'm going to take a break. I think I hear some hot cocoa calling me." With a wink at me she skated off, leaving me alone with Paul. I felt as if my security blanket was gone, and I wanted to kill her.

"So, are you a sophomore at Pine Ridge, Lindsey?" Paul asked. I was sure he was just making small talk to be polite.

"Uh—no." I cleared my throat. "Actually, I'm a junior."

He grimaced. "Sorry. Guess I just put my foot in my mouth."

"No, that's okay," I assured him quickly. "I mean, everybody thinks that when they first meet me. I guess it's because I'm so short."

Now Paul smiled warmly. "You know what they say, don't you?"

Confused, I stared at him. "What?"

"Good things come in small packages."

How was I supposed to respond to that? Karen would have come back with any one of a dozen clever comments, but not me. I just stood there, blushing, and probably looking like a giant tomato, as Luke would say.

I got the distinct impression that Paul was flirting with me. But why? He could have his pick of hundreds of attractive girls at Pine Ridge, yet here he was, flirting with short, red-faced me.

"Would you like to skate?" He held out his hand to me as the theme song from *Ice Castles* came over the rink's sound system.

I nodded numbly and slid my hand into his. We took off slowly, and I could tell that Paul was adjusting his long, powerful strides to

23

match mine. It was magic skating with him, and the song came to an end all too soon.

"Wow! You guys looked really good out there!" Karen exclaimed as we pulled up to the rink's entrance. I recognized the plotting look in her eyes and knew exactly what she was thinking. From the way she was glancing from me to Paul, I knew I'd better do something before she embarrassed me to death.

"Well," I said quickly, "I guess we'd better be going, right, Karen?"

Karen gave me a startled look. "Huh? Oh, yeah, I guess so. See you around, Paul."

As we stepped off the ice onto the rubber floor mats, I turned around. "It—it was nice seeing you again," I said to Paul.

"Yeah, you too. Maybe I'll see you at school tomorrow?"

I nodded, and started to walk away.

"Hey, remember those lessons," he called after me. "You're a wonderful skater."

I smiled shyly and hurried after Karen, who was returning her skates to the man at the rental counter.

"I think a certain Olympic skater is quite smitten with a certain petite redhead," she said, grinning at me.

"Smitten?" I repeated. "That sounds like a word my grandmother would use."

Karen rolled her eyes. "Never mind my choice of words. You know what I mean. I saw the looks he was giving you as you skated romantically around the rink." Karen batted her eyelashes and twirled around as if she were dancing.

"Karen!" I snapped. "Stop that! What if somebody's watching?"

"You mean like Paul?" Karen laughed. "Don't worry. I think Romeo left."

I glanced around the rink. Sure enough, Paul was nowhere to be seen. "Why would he leave so soon?" I wondered aloud. "He only just got here."

"I don't know. Maybe he went to the bathroom. Or maybe, when he knew that you were leaving, he just couldn't stand the thought of skating without you, so he left too."

"Oh, you!" I slapped her playfully on the arm. "Don't I wish!"

I sat down on a nearby bench and began to unlace my skates. "Do you really think he's interested in me?" I asked.

Karen sighed. "Yes, Lindsey, I really do. Why is that so hard for you to believe?"

25

"I don't know—it just is. I mean, he could have any girl. Why me?"

"Why *not* you?" Karen handed me my skate bag. "Really, Lindsey, it's a drag always trying to convince you what a nice, sweet, pretty person you are!"

I pulled off my skates and wiped the blades dry with a piece of terry cloth. "It's just that I never had a super guy like Paul show any interest in me before. I seem to appeal only to younger boys, like Trent."

Karen grinned. "Well, it looks like your luck just changed. I think you just hit the jackpot!"

A silly grin spread across my face as I thought about Paul—his eyes, his dimple, the way we had skated together. . . . "You know what, Karen?" I murmured. "I think you may be right."

Chapter Three

"So you're really taking lessons again, huh? I've never seen you so flipped out over a guy before," Karen said a week later as we got into her car.

I shuffled my history notes together and handed them to her. "I already told you, I'm not doing this just because of Paul," I said virtuously. "I really do want to improve my skating."

"Sure." Karen took the notes and grinned at me.

"Oh, okay," I admitted. "So maybe I *am* doing this to get closer to Paul. It's my only shot. Besides, the skating club is putting on an ice show this year and I'm going to try out for it. If I get a part, maybe Paul will *really* notice me."

Karen smirked.

"Just study the notes, okay?" I gave her a playful poke and picked up my skate bag. Tonight was my first lesson, and Karen was giving me a ride to the rink.

"Thanks for the ride, Karen," I said as we pulled up in front of the building a few minutes later. "I hope my parents will add me to their insurance policy next month, and then I'll have my own wheels—part of the time anyway."

"Hey, no problem," Karen said. "You know I don't mind. Call me later, okay?"

I nodded, and got out of the car. "Bye."

I waved and watched as she drove off. I was starting to feel nervous. I hadn't taken lessons in so long! What if I really wasn't that good? Or what if I never got any better than I was right now?

Taking a deep breath, I headed inside, working hard to calm my nerves. After all, this was what I really wanted, wasn't it? I loved to skate—just the sound of blades swishing over the ice excited me. I tried to tell myself that I'd be doing this even if Paul weren't in the picture, but I knew he had a lot to do with it.

I went to the locker room and sat down on a bench, exchanging my tennis shoes for the soft white leather boots of my skates.

As I was lacing them up, I heard footsteps behind me, and then a friendly voice called out, "Lindsey, hi!"

I looked up and saw Becky Williams smiling warmly at me. Becky was the kind of girl who always looked as though she had just stepped from the pages of some glamour magazine. Becky was not only blond and beautiful, she was also one of the most popular senior girls at Pine Ridge High. But even though you wanted to hate her for being so perfect, you couldn't because she was so nice.

"Hi," I mumbled, surprised that she knew who I was. We'd never even spoken before.

"Do you have class tonight?"

I nodded. "Do you?"

She grinned. "Yeah. I'm so excited! I've been taking lessons ever since I was little, but I took a few months off and now I'm really out of shape. I just need to brush up on some of the more difficult combinations, you know?"

I nodded as if I knew exactly what she was talking about. I didn't though. The last time I'd taken skating lessons was back in grade school. I only hoped that I didn't make a total fool of myself in front of her and everyone else.

I finished lacing up my skates and crammed my bag into the locker. As Becky followed me out to the rink, she said, "I'm really glad you're in my class. It's nice to know someone."

I was flattered by her comment. After all, we didn't really know each other at all, and Becky was a senior while I was just a lowly junior. I felt some of my nervousness start to fade away. *Who knows?* I thought. *Maybe Becky and I could become friends. Maybe she could even help me improve my skating.*

Feeling more confident, I pinned my locker key to my boot lace and joined the rest of the class out on the ice. There were about fifteen other kids, none of whom I recognized.

"Do you know anybody here?" I asked Becky.

She shook her head. "Not really. One of those girls was in one of my classes last year, but I don't recognize anyone else. What about you?"

"Not a soul."

Suddenly our instructor appeared out of nowhere, like a whirlwind. He was short but muscular, with curly brown hair and a friendly smile.

"Hello, everybody! For those of you who don't know me, I'm Shawn Carter. But please, call me Shawn."

"Oh, he's so nice! You'll really like him," Becky whispered in my ear. "I've had Shawn before."

"Some of you I recognize," Shawn continued, "and others are new to me. But I'm sure we'll all get along just fine." He glanced down at the clipboard he was holding. "In a minute I'll get each of your names. But before I do, I have a real treat for you."

We all perked up, wondering what our instructor had in store for us.

"I'd like to introduce you to someone who some of you may have already met or read about in the paper recently. He's a former Olympic skater turned pro who has graciously agreed to help me instruct this class."

Suddenly my heart began to beat so hard that I was sure everyone could hear it. I rubbed my palms against my thighs and tried to remain calm. It couldn't be, could it? Shawn couldn't be talking about . . .

". . . Paul Taylor!" he announced, and everyone began to clap as a tall figure swooped by us from behind and joined Shawn up front.

"Ohhh!" Becky squealed in my ear. "This is so cool!"

I nodded, too thrilled to say a word as Paul stood before us, flashing that dazzling smile. He glanced around the group as Shawn spoke, and suddenly his eyes met mine. And then he smiled.

"Oh, Lindsey," Becky exclaimed in a whisper, "did you see that? Paul just smiled at me!"

I didn't say anything. Let her think what she wanted. That smile was definitely directed at me, I was sure of it!

But I hardly had a minute to think about it. Shawn took our names, then split us into two groups, one taught by him and one taught by Paul. Becky and I were in Shawn's group, and he gave us the workout of our lives. I had never been more exhausted than I was at the end of that first class. Shawn had us all constantly moving, jumping, and twirling with hardly a chance to catch our breath. "Practice makes perfect" was his motto, and I had a feeling he was never going to let us forget it.

"Whew! What a workout! I'm bushed," Becky said, gliding up beside me when our lesson was over.

I nodded in agreement as we stepped out of the rink onto the rubber floor mats. "Yeah, but Shawn sure is good. I know I'm going to learn a lot."

"Oh, yeah, Shawn's great. He used to skate professionally, you know." Then she leaned toward me with a mischievous gleam in her eye. "But, boy, what I wouldn't give to have Paul coaching our group!"

"You know it!" I exclaimed.

I guess I should have been pleased to be in Shawn's group, since he was taking the more advanced group of skaters. But every time I looked across the ice and saw Paul working with his group, I wondered what it would have been like to be in it. I kept glancing over, hoping to catch him looking at me, but he was much too busy to notice me again.

"Is he cute, or what?" Becky sighed as we made our way to the locker room. "And he's in three of my classes at school!"

My head snapped up at Becky's statement. "*Three?* Paul Taylor is in *three* of your classes?"

Becky nodded, grinning widely. "Yeah. Pretty neat, huh?"

I opened my locker and took out my belongings. "Did you know that he was going to be here tonight?"

"No. Neither did anybody else, or you can bet that most of the girls at Pine Ridge High would have shown up!" She sat down and began unlacing her skates.

I did the same, sadly going over all the facts in my mind. Becky was a senior. Becky was beautiful. Becky was a great skater. And Becky had *three* classes with Paul. It was only a matter of time before he noticed her, and then where would that leave me? Out in the cold! I could never compete with someone like Becky.

"Well, guess I'll see you Thursday." She stood up, slinging her bag over one shoulder. "Bye, Lindsey."

Slowly, I finished unlacing my skates and carefully wiped the blades dry. I took my time, and when I finished, most of the students in my class were already gone or on their way out the door. I knew perfectly well that I was deliberately dawdling, hoping that maybe I'd run into Paul. But as I slung my skate bag over my shoulder and walked slowly down the main corridor, I didn't see him anywhere.

Disappointed, I made my way to the exit, and as I stepped outside, an icy wind hit me like a slap in the face. I shivered, gathering my coat closer around me, and headed for the pay phone near the door to call my mother and ask her to pick me up. As I fumbled in my pocket for the quarter I was sure was there, I suddenly remembered that I'd spent it that afternoon for a bag of chips at the school snack bar.

"Oh, rats!" I said aloud. I didn't have any other change, so I'd have to call collect. I was just about to place the call when I heard a voice behind me.

"Lindsey? Is that you?"

I turned and to my delight found myself face-to-face with Paul. He had on a bomber jacket with the collar turned up, and the wind was ruffling his hair.

"Hi," I said softly.

"Are you waiting for someone?" Paul asked.

"Yes—I mean, no. I mean, my mother is supposed to pick me up but I have to call her first and I don't have any change, so . . ." I began.

35

Paul stuck his hand into his pants pocket, found a quarter, and held it out to me. "Here—be my guest. But when you call home, tell your mom she won't have to come out in this cold, cruel weather." He broke into a grin. "Tell her that one of the nice, kind skating instructors will drive you home."

"Really?" I exclaimed. "Are you sure? I mean, you don't have to. I'm sure Mom won't mind picking me up."

"Lindsey, I know I don't have to," Paul said. "I'm offering only because I want to. Now, go ahead—call."

So I did. My mother okayed the ride home, and I hung up the receiver.

"Great!" Paul picked up his bag and stared toward the parking lot. "C'mon, my car's over there."

I followed him across the lot, my heart beating wildly. I couldn't believe this was happening! I was actually riding home with Paul Taylor!

We stopped in front of a shiny red BMW. "*This* is your car?" I asked as he opened the passenger door for me.

"Well . . ." Paul went over to the driver's side and slid in quickly behind the wheel. He put the key into the ignition and started the engine. "Not exactly," he said, his hazel eyes sparkling. "Actually, not at all. It's my sister's. Here—let me get the heat going." He adjusted some dials on the dashboard. "It'll be warm in just a second." He sat back and looked at me. "How about stopping for a cup of hot chocolate on the way home? I know this great little place not too far from here."

I lowered my lids, and then looked up at him from beneath my lashes, hoping I looked sweet and alluring. "Well . . ."

"I promise I'll behave." He smiled. "Well, what do you think? Are you going to throw caution to the winds and have a cup of hot chocolate with me?" he asked.

I grinned. "Why not? I've always wanted to live dangerously."

Paul eased the car through the parking lot and out into the traffic. "It's right down the street." He looked over at me and our eyes connected for just a second. I felt my heart skip a beat and wondered if I should pinch myself. Maybe it was all a dream. Maybe I would wake up any minute and this would turn out to be nothing but a great fantasy.

"Well, here we are." He pulled up in front of a quaint little shop with red checkered curtains at the windows. "Be prepared for the best hot chocolate you've ever tasted."

As we entered, the smell of pastries and coffee filled our nostrils.

"Isn't this place great?" Paul asked as the waitress seated us in a small booth. "It really reminds me of home."

This was my chance to get to know him. "And where is that?" I asked eagerly.

Paul leaned back. "Well, right now it's with my sister and her family here in Pine Ridge. But before this I lived with my mom in Seattle. That's where I grew up."

I gazed at him, admiring his strong, well-defined chin and wavy chestnut hair. "What about your dad?"

Paul said quietly, "He and my mom divorced when I was little. I don't see him much, although he did come and see me at the Olympics last year. He lives in Hawaii, with his new family."

"Hawaii!" I exclaimed. "How neat! Have you ever visited him there?"

Paul shrugged. "Yeah—once. I didn't feel very comfortable. I love my dad, and I know he loves me, but there's this big gap between us and—well, he's got a new family now, and I don't really feel like a part of it."

My heart ached for him. I was sorry I'd made him feel sad.

He continued. "You're really lucky, you know, having both your parents together. Not many kids do anymore."

I nodded. "Yeah, but sometimes I'd like to divorce my brother!"

That made him smile slightly. "I almost feel like an only child. My sister is ten years older than me. She's more like a second mother than a sister."

"How come you're living with her?" I asked.

Paul ran a hand through his hair. "Well, Mom decided to tour Europe this year with her cousin, and she didn't like the idea of me staying home all alone. So she suggested staying with my sister and finishing my education at a *real* school."

I was confused. "*Real* school? What does that mean?"

"Oh, you know—a public school. I've had a private tutor ever since I started skating seriously." He paused, fiddling with his napkin. "It's nice though, being here in a nice, normal, all-American school. Being a senior at Pine Ridge High is a great experience."

I made a face.

"No, I mean it!" Paul laughed at my expression. "It is! You know, sometimes I think I missed out on a lot. Sure, I got to see the world and experience different things, but normalcy is seriously underrated, if you ask me."

I smiled. "Trust me, I don't think you missed out on that much."

Just then the waitress came by to take our order, and returned a few minutes later with two steaming mugs of hot chocolate with little marshmallows floating on top.

"I hope I haven't bored you with my life story," Paul said almost shyly. "But you're a really great listener."

"Oh, I wasn't bored at all!" I exclaimed. "Believe me, I only listen when somebody has interesting things to say."

We sipped our cocoa in silence, and when I was almost finished, I looked up to find Paul gazing at me. Flustered, I crumpled up my napkin and glanced away.

"You know what I like about you, Lindsey?" he said.

I shook my head.

"Well, since we left the skating rink you haven't pulled out one of those stupid little compacts that most girls seem to carry around just to see what they look like. I hate it when girls do that. It's like they're more worried about how they look than who they're with."

I began to blush, and Paul laughed. "Hey, am I embarrassing you? I'm sorry. You look real cute when you turn all red like that."

I just shrugged and smiled.

"You know, we've talked an awful lot about me, but I haven't found out much about you, Lindsey. What's your story?" He pushed his empty mug aside and leaned his elbows on the table.

"My story?" I echoed. "I don't really have one. My life has been pretty—well, blah."

Paul shook his head. "I don't believe that. There's got to be more to Lindsey Matthews than meets the eye. Not that what meets the eye isn't pretty nice," he added.

I felt myself blushing again.

"What about skating?" Paul asked. "What got you interested in that?"

So I told him how my mom had taken

41

Luke and me skating way back when we were little kids. "I've loved everything about it ever since," I said. "You know—the look, the sound of blades cutting into the ice. . . ."

"I know the feeling," Paul said. "There's just something about the ice. If I stay away too long, I really miss it."

"That's exactly how I feel!" I exclaimed, thrilled to discover that we had this in common. "But the difference between us is that *you* skated in the Olympics and I only fooled around."

"True," Paul acknowledged. "But you might have done the same thing if someone had seen your potential and trained you."

"Oh, I don't think . . ."

Paul leaned across the table, staring directly into my eyes. "You're good, Lindsey. I watched you tonight during class. You've got a lot of talent."

I wasn't sure what to say then. Luckily, I didn't have to say anything because the waitress came up and laid our bill on the table.

"Well, I better get you home before your parents send the cops out after me," Paul teased as he glanced at his watch. He put some change on the table for a tip and then paid the cashier at the front counter.

"So, where exactly do you live?" he asked as we buckled ourselves back into his car.

I gave him directions and snuggled down into the leather seat, feeling secure and warm. It was so great being with Paul like this! I had to keep reminding myself that it was *not* a date. He was probably only being polite, happy to talk to someone else who shared his interests. I was sure he would have given Becky a ride home, too, if she'd been without a quarter. *Becky.* Now, why did I have to think about her at this moment? Just when I was feeling good too!

"You're awfully quiet. Is anything wrong?" Paul glanced at me, and I realized that my forehead had puckered into a frown.

"Oh, no. Not at all. I was just thinking."

"What about?"

"Nothing special."

"Okay, if you say so." He shook his head. "You know, Lindsey, you sure are different from any girl I've ever known."

Was that a compliment? I hoped so. It sure sounded like one anyway. My heart began to beat faster.

With disappointment I noticed we were turning down my street. I wished the ride could last forever.

"It's the second house—there, on the left, the one with the white mailbox," I said, and Paul pulled into the driveway.

He stopped the car and turned toward me. It was very dark, and the only sound was the gentle purring of the BMW's engine. "Thanks for letting me take you home," he said softly.

For a brief moment I wondered what it would be like if he wrapped his arms around me and held me close while I snuggled my head against his shoulder. What would it be like if he kissed me, his soft, full lips pressing against my own . . . ?

Flustered, I bent down to pick up my bag, then reached for the door handle. "Thank *you* for driving me," I said. "It was really nice of you. And thanks for the hot chocolate too."

Paul smiled and leaned closer, so close, in fact, that I thought he actually *would* kiss me. I held my breath.

"Lindsey—" He hesitated, and I hoped he was going to say something thrilling. But all he said was "You're welcome."

I forced myself to open the door and got out of the car. "Good night," I murmured.

As I went inside my house, my feet hardly seemed to touch the ground. Even though it was crazy, I knew I was head over heels in love with Paul Taylor.

Chapter Four

"Lindsey!" Karen exclaimed the next day. "Look at this!" She pulled me to such an abrupt halt in junior hall that one of my books fell to the floor.

"Jeez, Karen, watch out," I said, bending down to retrieve the book. We were on our way to third period, and I'd just given her a condensed version of my evening with Paul. Then I started to moan about how I never saw him outside of the rink. I was starting to feel pretty sorry for myself, when Karen just about ripped my arm out of the socket.

When I stood up, I noticed what she was staring at. I looked at the long strip of colored paper taped to the wall. I vaguely remembered walking by it for weeks, but I'd never paid any attention to it before. Now the long blue banner with fancy lettering seemed to jump out at me.

"The Winter Formal?" I asked. "What about it?"

"Don't you get it? The Winter Formal is one of the most important dances of the year!"

"I know that," I said. "You don't have to remind me. But I don't have a date, and—"

"Be quiet, and don't interrupt me," Karen interrupted. "If you go to this with Paul, romantic sparks just might ignite! You'll have found your true love, and—"

"Karen," I sighed, and shifted my books from one arm to the other. "I hate to burst your bubble, but you're forgetting one small detail."

"What?"

"How am I going to get Paul to ask me?"

Karen smiled. "You don't."

"But you just said . . ."

She gazed at me pityingly. "Lindsey, these are the nineties, remember? Girls don't have to sit around anymore waiting for guys to ask them out. So you invite Paul to the dance."

"You have got to be kidding!" I groaned. "Karen, that's the dumbest idea you've ever had."

"Why?" Karen said calmly. "What's the big deal? The worst he could say is—"

"No," I finished for her. "And I would absolutely die of humiliation if that happened! No way am I going to ask Paul Taylor to the dance. I'll just have to rely on my skating to get closer to him." I began to walk quickly away in the direction of our locker.

"But he might also say yes," Karen protested, hurrying after me. "Think of the romantic possibilities. You and Paul would make a great couple. Remember how you two skated together?"

"How could I forget?" I sighed dreamily.

"Exactly. Don't be a wimp, Lindsey. Just think what it would be like to dance with him all night!"

A warm, tingly feeling started at the tips of my toes and traveled all the way up my spine. It was only too easy to imagine myself twirling around in Paul's arms, looking up into his eyes, returning that adorable, dimpled smile. . . .

"Lindsey?" Karen glanced at me questioningly as she opened our locker. "What are you thinking?"

I handed her a couple of notebooks. "I'm thinking—well, I'm thinking that I just might do it."

Right before fifth period Trent Peterson caught up with me in the hall.

"Would you by any chance want to go to the Winter Formal with me, Lindsey?" he asked nervously.

I stared at him, too stunned to speak. I knew it was only a matter of time before he got up the courage to ask me out. But I'd never imagined it would be so soon, or that he'd invite me to a major event like this.

Before I could think of a reply, he continued hastily. "Look, you don't have to give me an answer right away. I don't mind waiting a few days. I know there are probably tons of guys wanting to go with you, but—well, I just had to ask. I'd be really honored if you said yes."

Honored? I stared at him, still speechless. I was really flattered, but I wasn't sure what to say. Trent looked so sweet and vulnerable with his curly blond hair and large blue eyes.

I didn't want to hurt his feelings, but he was only fifteen, for Pete's sake!

"Uh—thanks for asking me, Trent," I finally managed to say. "I'll let you know real soon, okay?"

Trent nodded eagerly and started down the hall just as Karen joined me at the library door. "Boy, is that kid nuts about you," she said as we went inside and sat down. "It's written all over his face. So, what did he want?"

I dropped my head onto the library table and moaned. "Oh, Karen, he asked me to the Winter Formal!"

"You're kidding!" Karen whispered, her eyes as big as saucers. "What did you say?"

"Nothing."

"You mean you didn't turn him down? You're not thinking of actually going with him, are you?"

I lifted my head. "No, but he was so sweet, and sincere, and—hopeful. I just couldn't say no to him right away. He's giving me a few days to think it over. What a mess!"

Karen leaned back in her chair. "Oh, come on, Lin, it's not so bad. You're blowing this way out of proportion. Look at it this way—if you can't get Paul to take you, you've always got Trent to fall back on." Grinning, she added, "Really, Lindsey, Trent's awfully cute. Wonder what he looks like in gym shorts?"

"Karen! Cut it out! This is a serious problem!"

Karen tried not to laugh. "No need to get hostile. Look, Lindsey, you can solve this whole thing by telling Trent that you've already got a date."

"But I don't!" I cried. "And I can't lie to him. I'd feel awful."

"Well then, do whatever you want. But right now we'd both better concentrate on our essays."

A while later I glanced up at the library clock in dismay. The period was almost over, and I hadn't gotten much of anything done. Quickly I piled my reference books on a cart by the checkout counter and gathered up my notes, along with my half-finished composition.

"See you after school, same time, same place?" Karen asked as the bell rang.

"Right—I mean, no!" I corrected myself. "I'm going straight over to the rink after sixth period. Tryouts for the ice show are this afternoon."

51

"Oh, yeah. I forgot about that. Well, good luck! See you later." She waved good-bye and disappeared into the crowd of students pouring out of the library.

I headed toward sixth-period geometry, but I couldn't really concentrate. By the time I finally arrived at the rink, I was a nervous wreck.

"Okay, people, listen up." Shawn greeted all the skaters with a smile when we had assembled on the ice. "It's great to see how many of you have turned out for the audition, and I'm sure you're all eager to find out what this year's production is going to be. So, I'm here to tell you."

Curiously, I glanced around at the thirty or so boys and girls waiting for Shawn's announcement. Some of them, like Becky Williams, I recognized from my lessons. The rest were from other classes. Paul was nowhere to be seen.

"As some of you may have heard, we're doing 'Snow White and the Seven Dwarfs.' " Several of the younger kids squealed and clapped in delight. Shawn smiled. "I think you'll all really enjoy it. The choreography is terrific." He glanced down at his clipboard.

"In a few moments I'm going to split you up into three groups—beginning, intermediate, and advanced, according to the classes you've been taking. Then I'll evaluate you in several different areas. Regardless of your individual levels, however, each and every one of you will have a part, whether it be Snow White herself, Dopey, or a tree in the forest." He paused a moment to scribble something down. "Paul Taylor and I will put our heads together after the tryouts and post the parts we have chosen for you by Monday. Unfortunately, there are no young men in this group tall enough or experienced enough to play the role of Prince Charming, so Paul will skate that part. Or should I have said 'fortunately' instead?" he added with a grin, and a few of the older girls giggled. "All right then, let's get this show on the road!"

Shawn proceeded to divide us into our appropriate groups, and then began to work with the beginners first.

I skated over to a far corner and began tracing some small figure eights. Several of the other advanced skaters soon joined me, nervously anticipating Shawn's evaluation.

"Can you believe it?" Becky exclaimed as

she glided up beside me. "We're going to be in a production with Paul Taylor! Isn't that just too good to be true?"

I nodded, trying to appear calm.

"I hear that the local cable station might televise the show on opening night!" a younger girl said excitedly.

"And we'll probably be on the evening news!" added another.

I wondered if it was true. Were we really going to be on television? My palms began to sweat at the thought of it. What if I got the part of Snow White? I could just picture myself stumbling, or, worse yet, falling for everyone in town to see. I shuddered. Was this what I wanted? Sure, it would be wonderful to skate opposite Paul, and I'd love to play Snow White. But what if I made a fool of myself? I tried to shake off the sick feeling in the pit of my stomach and concentrate on the exercises. *After all,* I thought, *I'll never be cast in the lead, so I don't really have anything to worry about.*

Finally Shawn had finished with the beginners and intermediates and made his way over to us.

"Relax, kids. This will be practically painless, I promise," he chuckled as he joined our group. "As I call your name, I want each of you to trace a figure eight, and then try the different combinations I give you. Don't worry if you don't get them right or can't do them all—just remember, every one of you will have a part. This is just a way for me to determine where your individual strengths lie and who would be best for each role, okay? Just skate your best and *don't worry*. Now, everybody back up against the boards and we'll begin." Shawn scanned his clipboard. "Tracy Kidder? You're on."

There were eight of us in my group, and I looked on with increasing nervousness as one by one each was called on to perform. I began to wish that somehow my name weren't on the list. On the other hand, I wanted to get my audition over with as quickly as possible. My one consolation was that Paul wasn't there. If he had been, I was sure I wouldn't be able to skate at all!

Suddenly Becky and I were the only ones left.

"Wish me luck," she whispered when her name was called.

Like she really needed it! Yet I found myself

holding my breath anyway as she executed a difficult jump and spin. Part of me wished she'd trip and fall, but the skater in me knew how wonderful it felt to take a difficult jump and make it. There was no other feeling like it. I let out a sigh of admiration when she finished her routine. Every one of her moves had been just perfect.

Now Shawn turned to me. "Okay, Lindsey, this is it, kid. Show me what you can do."

As Becky skated off to the side, I hesitantly moved out into the center of the ice. Taking a deep breath, I slowly traced a figure eight. It came out beautifully, one of the best I'd ever done, and I felt a little less nervous.

"Great, Lin, beautiful!" Shawn beamed his approval. "How about doing a camel sitspin for me? Then follow it with a double toe loop, a Salchow, and a double axel."

I nodded and gulped. There was that double axel again! I hated that jump with a passion. It was always so difficult for me.

I completed the camel sitspin and the first two jumps effortlessly. My heart was pounding wildly as I began to pick up speed. In a split second I hurled myself upward, twisting my body around. I spun the required amount of turns and then came down for a landing. That's when I almost lost it. It was a shaky landing, to say the least. I had pitched myself too far to one side and came dangerously close to losing my balance, but I didn't. I caught myself just in the nick of time and came to a slightly wobbly halt.

"Okay! Lindsey, that was great! Good job," Shawn said, and I sighed with relief.

I noticed him making notes on his clipboard, and I almost died of curiosity. How could I wait until Monday to find out what part I'd been assigned?

"You were really good, Lindsey. I wouldn't be surprised if you get the part of Snow White," Becky said, coming up beside me as we left the rink.

I stared at her in amazement. "You're kidding, right? I mean, did you see my double axel? It was horrible! I almost didn't make it."

"But you did," she said earnestly, "and that counts for a lot."

"Thanks, Becky." I smiled. "But you're the one who'll be playing Snow White, mark my words."

Becky grinned. "Well, I can't say that I would be disappointed. I could think of a lot worse things than skating in Paul Taylor's arms!"

"You said it!" I agreed, and we both laughed.

Becky was turning into a friend. I still wished she would do something to make me hate her, but it was nice to have someone to share my feelings with, even if she was my main competition.

"Well, guess I'll see you Monday, in front of the bulletin board," she said as we began taking off our skates.

"Yeah—just look for my name next to Dopey!"

Becky laughed. "I doubt that. You're a good skater, Lindsey. I wish you all the luck in the world."

Chapter Five

"Well, are you going in or not?" Karen demanded as we sat in her car in front of the skating rink on Monday afternoon. We both knew that the results of Friday's tryouts had been posted.

I hesitated. "I don't know, Karen. What if I've been cast as a tree or something?"

"Well, you'll never find out unless you go in and see, will you?" she pointed out.

I started to get out of the car very slowly.

"You want me to come in with you?" Karen offered.

I shook my head. "No. Just wait right there

and keep the engine running. I'm going to run in and out real fast!"

On shaky legs I jogged into the building and over to the bulletin board, my stomach churning. At least I was the only one there at the moment. I couldn't have handled seeing my name next to some dwarf's with everyone else around.

My heart sank and landed with a thud when I noticed Becky's name at the top of the list next to Snow White. *Oh, well,* I told myself sadly, *that's no big surprise.* Gathering up my courage, I looked to see which dwarf I was to play, but I couldn't find my name at all. I wasn't a dwarf or a forest animal, or even a tree. Confused, I started at the top again and there it was, right below Snow White and Prince Charming: Lindsey Matthews—Wicked Queen.

Shawn appeared suddenly from around the corner and gave me a friendly pat on the shoulder. "Congratulations, Lindsey. That's a difficult and demanding role, but Paul and I are sure you'll do well. I have great faith in you."

"Uh—thanks . . ." I mumbled, swallowing tears of disappointment.

I walked back outside in a daze, opened the car door, and slumped down in my seat.

"Well?" Karen asked eagerly. "Am I sitting next to Snow White, or what?"

I sighed. "Or what."

"Okay, so you didn't get the lead. What part *did* you get?"

I moaned.

"A dwarf, right?" Karen guessed. "Hey, being a dwarf isn't so bad. They're awfully cute, and they have lots of scenes."

"Karen," I replied, "I'm not a dwarf."

"Oh. Well, what are you? A tree?"

I shook my head.

"A bush? A bird? The poisoned apple?" Karen joked, and looked confused as I shook my head to every one of her suggestions. "I don't understand. What else is there?"

I moaned again. "Try the wicked queen who's really a witch!"

"Oh, right!" she exclaimed. "The one who does the 'mirror, mirror, on the wall' bit! I forgot all about her."

"Gee, thanks," I muttered. "Lucky me. I got stuck with the part that everybody forgets."

Karen held up a hand. "Now, wait a minute. I'm not everybody. Just because I forgot doesn't mean anyone else will. I'm sure you'll make a great witch—I mean, queen."

"Oh, Karen!" I cried. "This is *not* what I wanted to happen at all!"

"Life doesn't always go the way we planned," she said solemnly.

"Please, Karen, give me a break! I don't need you getting all philosophical on me."

"Sorry." Karen ran her fingers around the steering wheel. "Look, I know you wanted to play Snow White, but being the witch isn't all bad. Think about it, Lindsey. Without the witch there's no story, so you're a vital part of this whole production."

"But playing a witch just isn't romantic," I wailed. "When the queen turns into the witch, I'll have to wear an ugly costume, and an uglier face, and act mean and nasty. On the other hand, Snow White gets to dance in the prince's arms and wear a beautiful costume. Snow White gets kissed in the end. The witch *dies*! Which part would *you* rather play?"

Karen pretended to think a minute. "Actually, I'd prefer Dopey. He's cute and lovable, and makes everyone laugh. Kind of like me, huh?"

I shook my head and tried to smile.

"Look on the bright side," Karen urged. "The wicked queen is one of the bigger roles, right?"

I nodded. "Yeah. So what?"

"Well, a bigger role means more practice, and more practice means spending a lot more time on the ice. With Paul."

"But not in Paul's arms."

"So what? He'll see what a wonderful skater you are and what a great job you'll be doing with your role. And in the meantime, you can still ask him to the Winter Formal, right?"

I nodded reluctantly. "I guess . . ."

Karen smiled. "I know the perfect thing to cheer you up. Let's go get some ice cream! And while we're pigging out, we'll talk about the way to ask Paul to the dance."

After school the next day Karen dropped me off at the rink for my lesson. "So it's all set, right?" she asked brightly. "You go to your lesson, you ask Paul to the Winter Formal, he says yes, I pick you up, and then we spend all night talking about it. How does that sound?"

"I'd say that sounds great—if I were you," I replied. "But I'm not. I just don't see how I can walk right up to him and—"

Karen cut me off. "There you go again, always thinking negatively! Give yourself some credit, would you? You're pretty, you're talented, and he already likes you. What's the problem?"

"That's easy for you to say." I got out of the car.

"Lin, Paul's not perfect and unattainable. Just have a little faith in yourself, okay?"

I rolled my eyes as I shut the car door, and then headed inside.

"Hi, Lindsey!" Becky greeted me with a smile at the front entrance.

"Hi, Becky." I smiled back, intimidated as usual by her striking beauty. "Congratulations on getting the part of Snow White. I knew you would."

She blushed prettily. "Oh, thanks! I was really surprised. I thought for sure you were going to land it." I walked beside her in silence, but Becky kept on chattering. "I'm really excited about the show, aren't you? It's going to be so much fun. Can you imagine? I'll be skating opposite Paul Taylor. This is one of the best things that's ever happened to me!" She glanced over at me, and sobered. "Boy, here's stupid me, going on and on—I'm really sorry you didn't get Snow White, Lindsey. But the queen is a good part, too, you know."

I nodded. "Yeah, I think it'll be really challenging." Yuck! Was that me talking? It sounded so phony!

After we put on our skates we joined our group at the far corner of the rink. As usual, I kept an eye out for Paul, but he and Shawn hadn't arrived yet.

When they did, I felt my pulse quicken. It was the first time I'd seen him since our conversation over hot chocolate, and I wondered if he remembered it as well as I did. Paul was as handsome as ever, in a deep green sweater that brought out the green flecks in his hazel eyes, and his cheeks were ruddy from the cold. When he saw me, he smiled.

That did it. I knew then I had to ask him to the Winter Formal. If I didn't, I would never forgive myself.

"We're going to try something different today," Shawn said, calling us to attention. "I want you advanced students to work with Paul while I take the other groups. I think you'd benefit from some of the things he can teach you. Let's do it!" He clapped his hands

65

and gathered up the beginning and intermediate skaters while the rest of us followed Paul to the other end of the rink.

"Can you believe this?" Becky whispered. "We finally get to work with Paul. It's about time!"

He stood in front of our little group and grinned. "Shawn's been telling me what a great bunch of skaters you are, but I'd like to see for myself. Show me what you can do!"

And I had thought Shawn was tough! For the next hour Paul put us through the most rigorous training I'd ever had. At one point he asked for a volunteer so he could demonstrate proper foot and blade placement for one of the combinations. I began to edge forward, but Becky beat me to it. I shrank back and watched enviously as he touched her shoulders and calves, imagining that he was touching me instead. I got a warm, tingly feeling just thinking about it.

When Paul finished his demonstration, he said, "All right, now everybody try it. One at a time." He motioned to the girl closest to him, and I thanked my lucky stars that it wasn't me. I didn't have a clue about what he wanted us to do—I had been too busy daydreaming to pay attention.

After watching a few kids ahead of me, I relaxed a little, knowing that the double Salchow was a jump I did well.

By the time my turn came I felt almost confident. Paul smiled warmly and nodded, indicating that I was to begin. I circled him slowly a couple of times, building up enough speed for the jump. I willed myself to concentrate on nothing but the double Salchow, but as I began to jump I could feel myself lose control. My arms and legs flailed as I tried desperately to keep from falling, without success. My bottom hit the ice with a thud and I skidded to a halt near the wall. I stood up, too embarrassed to even look over at my group, much less at Paul.

"Are you okay, Lindsey?" he asked, and I knew that every eye was on me.

I nodded wordlessly.

"Good." Turning to the others, Paul said, "Now, that's exactly what we're trying to avoid. Can anyone tell me what Lindsey did wrong, and what she should have done differently?"

I skated to the rear of the group, my face flaming. Great! All I needed was having my horrible jump critiqued in front of everybody. Talk about humiliating! Why had I chosen this particular moment to mess up? I thought about my role in the ice show and had serious doubts about whether or not I would be able to go through with it.

"Hey, don't worry about it. Everybody falls now and then," Becky said kindly as she sidled up next to me. Of course, her jump had been textbook perfect.

I smiled slightly, wishing she would go away and leave me alone. I knew I should appreciate her friendship, but at that particular moment, her presence was driving me crazy. Her looks, her clothes, her moves—she didn't even seem to sweat!

I sighed, and brushed back a damp curl from my forehead, wondering how Paul felt about me now. It was pretty obvious that I cracked under pressure. Maybe he was doubting everything he had said about me being a talented skater. I knew I was. *But after all, Paul's a professional,* I told myself. *He must have fallen hundreds of times.*

Still, I couldn't help feeling more and more stupid every time I thought of flubbing the jump. And I was supposed to have the confidence to ask Paul to the Winter Formal? I almost laughed out loud.

I stole a sideways glance at Becky, noticing how engrossed she seemed to be in what Paul was saying. Then I let myself look at him. His eyes were sparkling and his face was animated as he spoke. He was so passionate about skating. As I listened to him intently, I soon found myself drawn into his excitement. I didn't even realize class was over until the group began to break apart.

"Wow, he is *so* good," Becky murmured.

I nodded, slowly coming out of the trance-like state I'd been in. I watched Paul skate over to talk with Shawn as I headed for my locker. While I unlaced my skates, I went over and over in my mind how I would ask him to the dance. By the time I had changed into my street clothes, my stomach was so tied up in knots that I thought I was going to throw up.

"So, got any big plans for tonight?" Becky asked as she picked up her bag.

"Not really . . ." I murmured, trying to keep an eye on Paul, who was just disappearing around a corner down the hall. I knew I'd better hurry if I was going to catch up with him. Turning back to Becky, I said, "I'm just spending the night with a girlfriend, Karen Anderson. Do you know her?"

"Oh, yeah, she's nice. Well, see you."

"Yeah—bye." I waited for a couple of seconds to let her get ahead of me, then took a deep breath. This was it. Now or never.

I hurried down the same hallway I'd seen Paul take just moments earlier. I wasn't sure where it led, and hoped I didn't end up getting lost. Suddenly it turned to the right, and I found myself standing in front of a door marked EXIT. I pushed it open and discovered that it led into a parking lot behind the rink.

It was dark outside, and there weren't many lights illuminating the lot. Still, I could make out Paul's figure unlocking the door to his car several feet away.

Suddenly a gust of wind seized the door behind me and slammed it shut. I saw Paul turn in my direction.

I wasn't sure what to do. Part of me wanted to run back into the building and forget the whole thing, and the rest of me wanted to get it over with. All of me just stood there, frozen to the spot.

"Lindsey?" Paul peered in my direction. "Is that you?"

"Uh—yeah, it's me." My voice cracked uncertainly.

He began to walk toward me. "What are you doing back here? This isn't a very safe place to be after dark. I'd hate for you to get mugged or something." He reached where I stood and stopped. "Do you need a ride home?"

I shook my head. Now what was I supposed to say? That I was following him because I wanted to ask him to the Winter Formal? "I—uh—got lost," I stammered. "I thought the hallway led someplace else and . . ." My voice trailed off uncertainly, and I wondered if I sounded as stupid to Paul as I did to myself.

The corners of his mouth turned up into a smile. "You sure you don't need a lift?"

"No. I've got a friend picking me up out front."

"Well, okay then. But at least let me walk you around the building."

We walked together to the front of the rink, where I spotted Karen's Bug idling near the main entrance.

"Well, here you are. Now, don't go traveling down any mysterious hallways in the future," Paul teased. "I just may not be around next time to rescue you."

I laughed, and felt myself relax a little. Then I remembered what I had to do.

"Paul, would you by any chance—that is, there's this dance at school next week and I know it's short notice but—would you—I mean, if you don't already have a date—would you like to go with me?" There! I'd done it! Awkwardly maybe, but I'd done it.

"You mean the Winter Formal?" he asked.

I nodded.

"Lindsey, I'd love to, but . . ."

My heart sank like a rock.

". . . I have to work. Shawn's given me a lot of responsibility for getting the Snow White production together, and I've been spending every free minute at the rink." He smiled sheepishly. "Not that I really mind. Skating's my life."

"I know." I gazed up at him, nearly drowning in the shimmering softness of his eyes. I forced myself to look away then. "Well, no harm in asking, right?" I glanced over at Karen's car. "I've got to go—my ride's waiting."

Paul nodded and I began to walk away.

"Lindsey?" he called after me.

I turned abruptly.

"I really am sorry—about the dance, I mean. It would have been fun."

I took a deep breath as I headed for Karen's

car. I had actually worked up the nerve to ask Paul Taylor to the dance! Yes, he had turned me down. Sure, I was disappointed. But even so, I felt better about myself than I had in a long time. Maybe I wasn't such a wimp after all.

Chapter Six

"**W**ell? What did he say?" Karen asked the following day, hovering beside me like a cat ready to pounce.

"He said he was really happy." I tried not to feel too depressed as I hung up the phone by my bed. I couldn't believe I had just let Karen talk me into calling Trent and accepting his invitation to the Winter Formal.

"That's great!" Karen cried. "You shouldn't be deprived of one of the biggest dances of the year just because Paul can't take you. We'll double-date. It'll be so much fun."

I shook my head. "Karen, I think I've made a big mistake."

"What do you mean?"

"Trent's going to think I really like him when I don't, at least, not the way he *wants* me to like him. And the last thing I want to do is hurt him."

"Of course you don't." Karen leaned closer to me. "But *he's* the one who asked *you* for a date, remember. All you're doing is accepting, no strings attached. If Trent expects every girl he goes out with to become his girlfriend, that's his problem. You're just out to have a good time at a dance, and there's absolutely nothing wrong with that." Karen nudged me playfully. "Besides, how do you know what might happen? He's no Paul Taylor, but he's cute and nice. Maybe you'll really hit it off."

"But I hardly even know him!"

"Dummy! That's what dates are for—to get to know each other. And even if no romance develops, at least you will have had a good time."

I sighed. "I don't know how you ever talk me into these things."

"Believe me, you'll be glad I did," Karen said smugly.

*   *   *

And so I went to the Winter Formal with Trent. Only it turned out that Karen was wrong. I wasn't glad I'd gone, and I didn't have a very good time. Doubling with Karen and Chuck was okay, and Trent was sweet, but all I could think about was Paul. And that made me feel guilty, because Trent all but tripped over himself, attending to me. I tried to at least pretend to be thinking about him, but it was no use. All night long I thought about Paul working so hard at the rink, and wondered what he was doing.

I soon found out.

We were on our way home from the dance, when Chuck's car pulled up to a stop sign at an intersection. I glanced out my window, and noticed Rose's Cafe on the corner. I thought about the cup of cocoa I'd had there with Paul, and wished for the hundredth time that it was Paul I was sitting next to, and not Trent. But as I happened to look into one of the windows at Rose's, my heart almost stopped.

Sitting at a table for two, deep in conversation with Becky Williams, was Paul. I got a horrible feeling in the pit of my stomach, and a huge lump formed in my throat. As Chuck drove on, Trent asked me a question, and somehow I managed to answer. But I couldn't manage to wipe out the image I'd just seen of Paul and Becky. It was all I could do to keep from crying.

Karen must have seen them, too, because she turned around from the front seat and shot me a sympathetic look.

"Call me in the morning, okay, Lin?" she said softly when we pulled up in front of my house.

Trent started to get out of the car and walk me to my front door. That was the last thing I needed, so I said quickly, "No—please, stay here. I'll see myself in. Thanks for the lovely evening, Trent. I had a nice time." I choked out the words and then flew up the driveway.

"C'mon, Lin, cheer up. Maybe it isn't what it looked like," Karen said the next morning when I called her. "Maybe they just ran into each other there."

"At ten o'clock at night? And Paul said he had to work, remember?" I said miserably. "He turned me down for the Winter Formal because of all the work he has to do on 'Snow White.'"

For once Karen had nothing to say.

"Maybe," I continued, "Paul and Becky had this date all planned and he just didn't have the guts to tell me the truth, so he lied about having to work, thinking I'd never find out. How about that?"

"And maybe they're just friends," Karen suggested, but I noticed the uncertainty in her voice. "Or maybe Paul went to Rose's when he was through at the rink and he just happened to run into Becky." Neither of us said anything more for a moment.

"So, what are you going to do today?" she asked at last. "Aside from moping around, I mean."

I shrugged. "Nothing, I guess. Except I've got rehearsal at three."

"Rehearsals on Saturday?" Karen sounded surprised. "I thought they were only once a week, between your lessons."

"They were, but Shawn decided we needed more practice if we were ever going to be ready by opening night, so he tacked on another day. Only now I'm thinking . . ."

"What?"

Taking a deep breath, I mumbled, "I'm thinking of quitting the production."

"Lindsey!" Karen exclaimed. "You can't be serious! You've got one of the lead roles."

I fiddled with the phone cord. "Well, I never was too thrilled about being cast as the wicked queen, and performing in front of all those people, maybe even on television, makes me want to throw up. The whole reason I tried out for the show was to impress Paul. But now that he and Becky are going out . . ."

"Hey, hold it," Karen cried. "You don't know that for sure. Besides, what if they are? You're not a quitter, Lindsey—at least you never used to be. Hang in there and prove to yourself and everybody else that you can do it. You mustn't let your fear of being in the spotlight or this thing with Paul and Becky get you down."

"That's easy for you to say," I complained. "You've had lots of boyfriends, and you've never been afraid of anything in your life! Remember last month when I had to give an oral report in English and I had to sit down because I got so dizzy I almost passed out? What if the same thing happens on opening night of 'Snow White'?" I shuddered. "I don't know why I thought things might be different now. It's just as hard. Actually, it's worse. I must have been nuts to try out in the first place."

"Lindsey Matthews!" Karen's voice was shrill. "I don't want to hear any more nonsense about you quitting the production! You may not be able to see all your potential, but I do, and so do lots of other people—Shawn, for one, or he wouldn't have given you a big part. You can't let him down now!" Her tone softened. "I'll help you all I can, Lindsey, honest I will. I can't do anything about your stage fright—only you can deal with that. But I'll give you all the moral support in the world, I promise."

"Why?" I asked. "Why is this so important to you? It's just a stupid ice show, that's all."

Karen groaned. "Don't you see? You've got the talent to do something really well, but you're letting your insecurities stand in the way. Do you know how many times I've wished that I could do anything as well as you skate? And now you want to give it all up just because you're afraid you *might* fail, and because you think Paul *might* be going out with Becky. Does that make any sense at all?"

I hesitated. Deep down inside I knew it

didn't. I'd always had visions of doing something great with my skating. Truthfully, I couldn't picture my life without it. As for Paul, I had to admit that there was nothing real between us, just my dreams of romance.

"C'mon, Lindsey—please? Don't wimp out," Karen begged. "You can do it, I know you can!"

I unraveled the phone cord from around my fingers. "Okay," I said at last. "I'll hang in there. But I'm really going to need all the moral support you can give."

I could almost see Karen grin. "Terrific! Everything's going to work out, just you wait and see!"

Chapter Seven

The next two weeks flew by in a blur. If I wasn't at school or frantically cranking out homework, I was at the rink. Skating lessons, "Snow White" rehearsals, and practicing on my own took up every free minute.

Rehearsals were grueling. More than once I came home with sore muscles and an aching heart, ready to throw in the towel. But true to her word, Karen came to every single rehearsal, encouraging me and keeping up my spirits, almost like my personal coach.

But as difficult as rehearsals were, working with Paul was even worse. When I had promised Karen that I'd hang in there, I had also promised myself to put as much distance between Paul and me as possible. It was the only way I could concentrate on my skating, and to ignore the pain he had caused me. I avoided eye contact with him as much as possible, and hurried away whenever he came toward me. I tried to convince myself that it would be easy to lose that special feeling I had for Paul, but it wasn't, even though I was sure it was Becky he really wanted.

I couldn't help watching their every move as they practiced their scene together—the tender way he held her, the look in his eyes. There was no way I could ever compete with Becky. She was too pretty and too competent, everything I was not. I tried to ignore the fact that they often arrived and left the rink together. They made the perfect couple, on and off the ice.

"Okay, people, that's enough for today," Shawn's voice boomed out across the ice on Friday afternoon. "Can I have a quick meeting with the dwarfs over here, please?"

Somebody clicked off the taped music we had been using, and the rink was silent except for the sound of blades swishing across the ice as seven small skaters hurried to Shawn's side.

I skated toward the exit, where Karen stood waiting for me as usual.

"You were terrific, Lin!" she enthused. "I'm really impressed."

As we headed for my locker, I shrugged, rubbing a stiff shoulder. "It's not all that great an accomplishment. I didn't do anything really challenging today." Then I flashed her a grateful smile. "But thanks anyway."

I was drying the blades on my skates, when I heard footsteps approaching us from behind. Karen straddled the bench beside me and whispered. "Don't look now, but . . ." Her voice dwindled off, but I could tell by the look in her eyes that it had to be Paul.

Quickly, I tucked a few stray strands of damp hair behind my ear and tried to calm my racing heart. What could I possibly say to him? What could *he* want to say to me?

"Hi, Lindsey."

I turned around on the bench, hoping I looked surprised. "Oh, hi, Paul."

Smiling down at me, he said, "I just wanted to let you know what a great job you've been doing with your part. Shawn and I were discussing how impressed we both are with your performance. Your skating seems to improve every day."

"Thanks," I replied as casually as I could. "I've been giving it a lot of effort."

"Well, it's paying off. You look real good out there."

I tried desperately to think of something clever to say, but my mind was a total blank. Karen wasn't any help at all—she was pretending to be busy looking for something in my locker. So I just sat there, smiling at Paul, feeling like an idiot.

"Well, I guess I'd better be going," he said at last, breaking the awkward silence. "And if you ever need a ride, don't hesitate to ask."

"Thanks. But I won't. Need a ride, I mean," I replied. "I can drive now. My parents just added me to their insurance policy." For the first time I wished they hadn't.

"That's great." Paul didn't make a move to leave, and I wondered if by some small chance there was something else he wanted to talk to me about.

"Paul? Oh, there you are!" Becky breezed up just then, her complexion glowing from her workout, yet every golden strand of hair perfectly in place. "I've been looking all over for you! I'm so glad I caught you before you left. Does your offer for a ride home still stand? If so, I need one after all."

Instantly, I felt as though I'd been socked in the stomach. Apparently Paul had offered me a ride only because Becky had turned him down. I was angry at myself for believing, if only for a moment, that Paul really wanted to spend some time with me.

Becky turned to me and smiled. "Hi, Lindsey! You've been doing a really great job with the wicked queen," she said enthusiastically. "Too bad we don't have more scenes together. I'd love to skate with you more often."

Yeah, right, I thought. I had a hard time believing that was true. After all, Becky had a wonderful romantic scene with Paul. Why on earth would she want to skate with anyone else?

"Thanks," I mumbled as I put my skates into my bag.

"Well, see you around, Lindsey. Bye, Karen." Paul waved, and I watched enviously as Becky followed him out of the room.

"Don't say it," Karen ordered, handing me my jacket. "I know exactly what you're thinking."

"What?" I asked innocently.

"You know what. You're wearing your

'wicked witch' face, Lindsey. Get a grip and don't let Paul and Becky get to you. You've been doing so well up till now!"

I pulled on my jacket. "It's just that for a minute there, I almost thought he—it seemed like—"

"Yeah, I know," Karen interrupted gently. "But try to forget it, Lin. If Paul really likes you, he'll find a way to let you know. And if he doesn't, you still have your skating."

We rushed out into the freezing night and I slid behind the wheel of my parents' car as Karen got in the passenger side.

After we buckled our seat belts, I eased out into the traffic and changed lanes very carefully. Rush hour was at its peak, and the streets were jammed.

"You're kind of quiet. Do you want to stop for ice cream or anything? It might pep you up a little," Karen suggested.

I shook my head. "No, I better not. My mom has dinner waiting. Besides, I've still got a lot of homework to tackle for next week."

"Okay," Karen said. "Call me tonight when you get to your English assignment. I don't understand the part about prepositional phrases and . . ."

Karen rambled on, but I didn't hear her because all of a sudden I caught sight of something small and furry bounding off the sidewalk and directly in front of my car.

Karen saw it too. "Lindsey! Watch out!" she screamed, bracing her hands against the dashboard.

In a split second I slammed on the brakes, missing whatever it was by inches. Before I could catch my breath, I heard the squealing of tires behind me and felt the impact of something crashing into us.

For a moment Karen and I just stared at each other.

Karen regained her voice first. "Oh, my gosh! Lindsey, are you okay?"

"Yeah, I think so." Gingerly I touched my shoulder and chest, where the seat belt had made a painful impression. "Are you?"

Karen nodded. My first thought was it was a good thing we were wearing our seat belts. My next thought was about the people in the other car. And also how badly was the other car damaged?

"At least you didn't hit whatever ran across the road. What was it anyway?" Karen asked shakily.

"I don't know," I replied. "It all happened so fast! I think it might have been a cat." I bit my lip. "What do I do now?"

"I think you're supposed to exchange insurance information with the other driver." Karen opened the glove compartment and began to rummage around for the necessary papers.

There was a frantic tapping on Karen's window, and we looked over to see an elderly woman peering in. In her arms she held a wriggling brown terrier in a plaid sweater. "Excuse me! Excuse me—are you all right?"

Karen rolled down her window. "Yeah, we're okay. But we don't know about the other driver yet."

"Don't worry. Everyone seems to be fine," the woman said. "And a young man passing by ran to a pay phone and called 911. The police should be here any minute. And I just want you both to know that I accept full responsibility for what happened. I'll stay until the police arrive and explain everything. If only Muffy hadn't wriggled out of his collar—To think that he could have been killed—oh, I'm so grateful that nothing happened to him!" Tears filled her eyes, and her voice quavered.

"I'm glad your dog's all right," I managed to

choke out. I couldn't believe I'd been driving my parents' car only two weeks, and I'd already had an accident. What would my folks say? What would the police say?

I didn't think things could get any worse, but I was wrong.

"At least your car doesn't look too badly damaged," the woman went on. "But the car behind you sure took a beating. It always happens to those expensive foreign cars, wouldn't you know!"

Oh, great, I thought to myself. *What kind of car am I involved with? A Mercedes? Porsche? Jaguar?*

"Uh-oh . . . !" Karen's voice trailed off as she turned to look out the rear window. "Isn't that Paul's BMW? And isn't that Becky behind the steering wheel?"

I whipped my head around so fast that I yelped when a sharp pain shot up my neck. But I felt even worse when I saw that Karen was right. That definitely was Becky on the driver's side, but where was Paul?

The thought had no sooner entered my mind than there was a tap on my window. Paul and I stared at each other as I rolled down the window.

"Lindsey!" Astonishment was clearly written all over his face. "I didn't know this was your car!"

"Actually, it's my dad's," I said weakly.

Nervously, he brushed a hand through his hair. "Man, my sister is going to *kill* me!"

I swallowed around the lump in my throat. "Are you okay?"

"Yeah, but the front end of the car looks like an accordion, and Becky's ankle is hurt pretty bad."

"Oh, no!" I gasped.

"Yeah. She wanted to drive so badly, and she kept begging me, so I let her just this one time. I never should have done it. Now she thinks she might have broken her ankle."

"Oh, Paul, I'm so sorry," I murmured.

"Me too." He shook his head. "If you hadn't slammed on your brakes like that, maybe she could have avoided running into you."

I got the feeling that he was blaming me, and I was so upset that I didn't know what to say.

"Hey!" Karen put in. "It was an accident! A little dog ran right out in front of us. What was she supposed to do? Run over it?"

Paul looked uncomfortable. "I'm not saying

91

it's Lindsey's fault. I just said I wished she hadn't put the brakes on so fast, that's all."

"Yeah, right!" Karen rolled her eyes in disgust.

I could feel the tears streaming down my cheeks. Having Paul blame me for an accident that I couldn't have avoided hurt so much, I didn't think I could stand it. And if Becky's ankle was really broken, I'd never forgive myself.

Suddenly the police and an ambulance arrived, and everything turned into a big commotion. The elderly woman explained everything to the police and claimed full responsibility. I handed over my proof of ownership and insurance papers, and my driver's license, feeling like a common criminal.

I gave my version of what happened to a policeman who scribbled down my story and Karen's statement in his notebook and then let us go. A couple of paramedics asked Karen and me some questions, then suggested we come to the hospital for X rays, just in case.

Paul and Becky went through the same routine, only Becky ended up on a stretcher in the ambulance.

* * *

"Lindsey, are you awake, dear?" Mom asked softly, coming into my room the next morning.

I yawned and stretched, wincing at the slight soreness of the muscles across my back and chest. I tried to focus on her as I rubbed the sleep from my eyes. "What time is it?"

"Almost ten." She opened the curtains at my window, flooding the room with sunlight. "How are you feeling?"

"Okay. A little sore, I guess. But Becky . . ."

I couldn't finish the sentence. I'd never forget the look on Paul's face in the hospital when he'd told me that Becky's ankle had been fractured. She would have to stay off it for the next six weeks, which meant there would be no ice show. I knew how disappointed Shawn would be. He'd probably be furious at me, too, because maybe in a way the accident had been partly my fault.

"Honey, you got a phone call a little while ago. It was your skating instructor," Mom said, and I cringed.

"Shawn?" I asked anxiously. "What did he want?"

"Apparently, he heard about the accident and wanted to see how you were feeling."

"And?" I propped myself up on one elbow.

"And," Mom said, "I told him you were fine, except for some minor bruises. He also wanted to know if you'd be making it to rehearsal today, and I told him it was up to you."

"Rehearsal?" I repeated. "But I thought—I mean, I just assumed that they'd cancel the show. Becky—you know, the girl who broke her ankle—has the lead role. I don't see how we can go on without her."

Mom picked up some clothes from the floor and draped them over a chair. "Perhaps he found someone to replace her."

I thought about that for a moment. Maybe Shawn knew somebody from outside our club who had agreed to take over Becky's part.

"So," she continued, "are you going to do it?"

"Yeah, I guess. . . ."

Mom looked at me closely. "Are you sure you feel up to it?"

I nodded. I was suddenly feeling much better. If the production didn't have to be canceled after all, maybe Shawn—and Paul—wouldn't be so mad at me.

"Well then, I guess you'll have to see if Luke or Karen can give you a ride. Your father's taken the car to get some repair estimates for the insurance company."

"Does it look bad?" I asked worriedly.

Mom shook her head. "No, not at all. From what I heard, the other car really got the worst of it."

I groaned inwardly as Paul's stricken expression flashed before my mind's eye again. He had acted really cold at the hospital, and it was obvious how concerned he had been for Becky. So was I, of course. I felt terrible, and I couldn't blame him for being angry at me. I didn't feel much like seeing him just yet, but the rehearsal began at one, and I had to be there, if only to find out how Shawn was going to proceed with the show.

"Lindsey? Can I see you in my office, please?" Shawn asked as soon as I arrived at the rink.

"Oh, sure. Just a second." Hastily, I put my belongings away, wondering what he wanted to see me about. Was he going to yell at me about the accident? Paul had probably already told him all about it, and I hoped he hadn't made it sound as if it had been *totally* my fault.

Shawn smiled as I entered his office. "Sit down, Lindsey. How are you feeling?"

"Fine. A little stiff though." I sat down carefully in the old overstuffed chair across from his desk.

"Well, I'm glad that's the only problem." His smile faded. "It's a shame that Becky was hurt. Aside from everything else, it does throw a slight kink into our production."

I stared at him. A slight kink? When Becky had the largest, most difficult role of all?

"However," he continued, "that shouldn't be too hard a problem to solve. Not with your skating ability and a little extra practice."

I wasn't sure what I was hearing. Did he mean what I thought he meant? "Uh—Shawn, I'm not sure . . ."

He leaned across his desk and looked squarely into my eyes. "I want you to take over the role of Snow White."

"Are you serious?" I gasped.

"I sure am." Shawn sat back in his chair and placed his fingertips together. "I've been watching you, Lindsey, and you have what it takes."

"But—but . . ." I sputtered. "I'm not good enough! Not for the lead role!"

"I happen to think you are."

"But what about my other role? What about the wicked queen? Who'd play her?"

"Tracy Kidder has already agreed to take it on, providing *you* agree to play Snow White. She's one of the forest animals now, but like you, she's improved greatly over the last few weeks."

"Gee, Shawn, I'm really flattered, but I'm not sure I can handle the lead role. I get really scared in front of large crowds of people and—"

"Everybody gets nervous," Shawn said calmly. "It's perfectly natural."

"But—but what about Paul? He might not want me for a partner," I blurted out. I couldn't say what I was really worried about— that I didn't think I could work closely with someone I cared for so much and was trying so hard to forget.

Shawn smiled. "I've already discussed it with Paul this morning, and he has no objection."

My mind went blank. I had no more excuses or reasons for why I shouldn't take over Becky's role. But what if I blew it? And how could I ever face Paul again after what had happened last night?

"Lindsey," Shawn said when I remained silent, "I can't force you to do this, and I'm not going to beg you either. But there are a lot of kids out there who have been busting their butts for this production, and they would be terribly disappointed to see it called off. I know you can do it. What do you say?"

He was right, of course. If I refused, I would be letting a lot of people down. And yet I didn't think it was fair that the whole thing rested on my shoulders.

Still . . . I licked my lips and cleared my throat. "Okay," I said at last. "I'll try it."

"Good girl!" Shawn stood up and grinned at me. "You're going to do just fine, Lindsey."

I wondered what I had gotten myself into. Shawn had a lot more confidence in me than I had in myself!

Chapter Eight

"Ever since the Winter Formal, Trent keeps asking me about you," Karen told me as she drove me home from school on Monday. "Now that you're playing Snow White, he even wants to come to practice with me and watch you rehearse."

"Oh, terrific," I groaned.

"He's really a nice guy, Lin. Why don't you give him a chance? He's bright, and sweet, and cute. I'd go out with him myself if he weren't so hung up on you," Karen admitted.

"But *I'm* not interested in *him*!" I reminded her.

"True," Karen acknowledged. "Not now anyway. But what if somewhere down the road you decide you *do* like him? Then what?"

I shrugged. "I doubt that will ever happen."

Changing the subject, Karen said, "By the way, you never did tell me how rehearsal went on Saturday. Did you finally get to dance in the arms of Prince Charming?" She fluttered her eyelashes at me.

"Ha, ha, very funny. Prince Charming hasn't spoken to me since the accident." I sank back against the seat and stared gloomily out the window. "Shawn's having me work on all the other scenes first, since there's so much to learn. Then, when I've got those down, he's going to have me get together with Paul."

"Too bad you have only one scene together."

I sighed. "Not really. The fewer, the better. The way things have been going, it's kind of a relief."

Karen said, "Maybe he's just really busy, what with helping produce 'Snow White' and all."

"Oh, sure. And maybe he just hates the sight of me!"

"Hey, don't be so depressed," Karen said gently.

"I can't help it." I sighed again. "Everything's starting to overwhelm me, Karen. I just don't see how I'm going to learn all Becky's skating sequences in only three weeks. And if I can't, the production will be a disaster."

"Well, that's not going to happen," Karen said confidently. "You'll learn them and you'll be fabulous. And then, when you're a famous skating star, I can say, 'I knew her when!' "

"Ha!" I said. "I wouldn't hold my breath if I were you."

We pulled up in front of my house, and as I collected all my stuff, Karen said, "You sure you don't want to do anything right now? We could go out for pizza or something."

I shook my head. "Thanks, but I've got tons of homework. Not to mention, I have to go to . . ."

". . . the rink." Karen finished my sentence for me. "I know, I know. You'd think I would have learned by now that you have absolutely no free time."

"Hey, it's all your fault, remember?" I pointed out. "You're the one who said I should go for it."

101

Karen held up her hands in defeat. "True. But how could I have guessed I was creating a monster? It seems like all you do is rehearse."

"I know," I agreed. "But I have so much to learn, and there's so little time. I have to practice every chance I get."

Karen nodded and waved good-bye as she drove off.

I spent the next hour and a half frantically trying to finish as much homework as possible. By the time I got ready to leave for rehearsal, my mind was swimming with history dates, geometry theorems, and French verb conjugations. I wasn't sure if I'd be able to remember how to put my skates on!

"See you later, Mom," I said as I grabbed the car keys from the kitchen counter. "I'll be back in a couple of hours."

She threw me a concerned look. "Are you sure you don't want me to drive, dear?"

"No, Mom, that's okay. I'll be really careful, I promise."

"I know you're always careful, Lindsey. I'm not worried about that. But aren't you maybe just a little frightened? After all, the accident was just three days ago."

I thought about that for a minute, and

realized that I was much more nervous about seeing Paul than I was about driving again.

"Not really, Mom," I said, then added, "To tell you the truth, the production scares me a whole lot more!"

She gave me a hug. "Your father and I are really proud of you, honey. Try not to worry. I'm sure you'll be wonderful when opening night comes."

I hugged her back, then headed for the rink. Just as I was pulling into the parking lot, I saw a girl on crutches hobbling toward the entrance of the rink. It was Becky, and Paul was right beside her.

Instantly, my heart sank. What was Becky doing here anyway? The last thing I needed right now was to have her watch me skating what should have been her role. I felt bad enough about the accident as it was, without her eyeing my every move. I waited until she and Paul had gone inside, then picked up my skate bag and followed.

As soon as I had put on my skates, I went out on the ice with the others and waited for Shawn to join us. A few minutes later he did, followed closely by Paul.

Rehearsal started, and every few minutes I'd glance up in the stands and catch a glimpse of Becky. Each time I did, it made me feel worse. I desperately wanted to tell her how sorry I was that this had happened, but I got a queer, sick feeling in my stomach whenever I thought about it. She'd always been so sweet and friendly to me before the accident, but now I wouldn't have blamed her if she said something mean and horrible to me in front of everyone. If she did, I knew I would probably burst into tears on the spot.

The rehearsal went fairly smoothly, considering how many other things I had on my mind besides skating. When Shawn finally called it quits, I practically flew off the ice.

I was on the way to my locker when I heard an unexpected voice. "Wow, Lindsey, you were terrific!"

Trent seemed to appear out of nowhere, followed by Karen. They were both beaming.

"Yeah, Lin, you were great. You make a perfect Snow White," Karen said.

"Thanks," I muttered, not knowing what else to say. I couldn't believe that Trent had actually showed up. "I thought you'd decided not to come. I didn't see you." I directed my remark to Karen.

"We sat up real high so we wouldn't disturb your concentration," Trent explained. "You're a really good skater."

They both seemed so sincere that, for the first time in days, I felt as though I might be making progress. Looking at Trent, I noticed his expressive blue eyes and the way his hair curled in little ringlets at his temples. He *was* good-looking, and he was awfully nice.

Just then I happened to glance to my right, in time to see Paul leaning over the railing to talk to Becky. They were both smiling, and I wondered what they were saying. They looked so close and cozy, as if they were sharing an intimate secret.

Then Paul looked over at me, and that's when I made up my mind. After all, Paul had Becky. Why shouldn't I have someone too? I'd show him that it didn't matter to me who he was dating or if he ever spoke to me again. He'd see that I wasn't just going to sit around pining away for him. And just maybe I could even make him a little bit jealous.

So while he was still watching, I gave Trent

my most dazzling smile. "How would you like to go out for pizza?" I asked.

"Sure!" Trent exclaimed eagerly. "I'd love to!"

"Yeah, me too," added Karen, giving me a funny look. "But I thought you had all this homework to do."

I smiled at Trent again. "It can wait," I said.

Chapter Nine

For the next two weeks I pushed myself harder than I ever had before. Trent showed up at the rink often, sometimes several days in a row. And Karen came, too, giving the moral support she had promised.

I made a major effort to make sure that Paul saw me with Trent as often as possible. I flirted with Trent shamelessly, and I wasn't positive, but I began to think it was getting to Paul. More than once I thought I saw him scowl when he caught sight of Trent and me.

But it got a lot more complicated once Paul and I started rehearsing our one big scene together. The tension between us seemed to be building daily.

"Wake up, Lindsey! That was supposed to be a double toe loop, not a single!" Paul exclaimed one afternoon when I had messed up and skidded across the ice on my bottom.

Gingerly, I picked myself up. "Sorry," I mumbled.

"Sorry isn't going to cut it," he snapped. "You've got to concentrate."

Hot tears welled up behind my eyelids. No matter how much I told myself that it didn't matter what Paul thought, it did. It mattered a whole lot. And it bothered me that it still bothered me. This was the first time he had ever yelled at me, and it hurt.

"I *am* concentrating," I said defensively.

"I don't think you are," Paul said, hands on his hips. "If you want to skate well, and I mean *well*, you've got to put everything else out of your mind and think about nothing but your skating."

"I said I was sorry! What else do you want from me?" Against my will, a tear slid down my cheek.

"Maybe," Paul continued, his eyes throwing daggers, "if you quit thinking about your boyfriend all the time, you might stop messing up so much."

My face burned at the mention of Trent. In a way, it was true. I *had* been thinking a lot about him, but not in the way Paul meant.

"It's really none of your business who or what I think about, is it?" I shot back.

Paul was about to retort when Shawn called out to us, "Okay, kids, take a break. I can see you both need one."

I sat down on a bench next to Paul, leaving at least five feet between us. Shawn came over to me and reached out to pat my knee.

"Lindsey, you're going to be fine. Really. Just loosen up a little, okay?"

I stared at my tightly clasped hands through blurry vision, willing myself not to cry. "I'm sorry about that last jump," I murmured. "I'll try to do it right next time, honest."

Shawn smiled at me sympathetically. "This has been an extremely difficult role to learn in such a short time, and you're doing a great job. Right, Paul?"

"Right," Paul mumbled, not meeting his eyes.

"I'm sure Paul's sorry for getting a little short-tempered. Right, Paul?" Shawn asked again.

Paul swallowed, and glanced over at me. "Yeah. I'm sorry, Lindsey."

"That's better." Shawn smiled benevolently at us both. "Listen, kids, I understand how you feel. The pressure is on. After all, opening night is just a week away. But I have complete faith in the two of you. Believe me, you're going to pull this off."

I felt my stomach knot up at the mention of opening night. I wished I'd never agreed to take Becky's part, but there was no way I could quit now. It was too late. Fliers and radio announcements about the production had been out for weeks, and the local cable channel had already announced that it was filming our first performance live. Tickets were selling at a good rate, the proceeds going to a local charity. There was no way I could avoid it, unless, like Becky, I was so badly injured that I was unable to skate.

"All right, let's give it another try," Shawn said. "Take it from the top." He motioned us back out on the ice and pointed a finger at his temple. "*Concentrate*, Lindsey. You can do it, I know you can."

With a pounding heart I headed for the center of the rink, willing myself to think of nothing but my skating. The music started and we began our routine.

With my eyes shut I lay perfectly still on top of the wooden box that on opening night would be transformed into Snow White's golden casket. Paul circled me several times. I could hear the blades of his skates cutting into the ice as he came closer and closer.

My heart beat even faster as I waited. The script called for him to kiss me, awakening me from the witch's spell. As yet, he never had. At each practice he would lower his head to mine, but no kiss. I wondered if that was what he had in mind for the actual performance. If he did, I couldn't blame him. After all, how could you kiss someone you were mad at?

And then I suddenly felt warm lips pressing gently against my own. In that instant my eyes flew open and I saw Paul's face close to mine. For a brief moment we gazed at each other. Then, very gently, he took my hand and pulled me to my feet. We began our romantic dance on the ice.

It was so easy to let the music carry me away. Every time Paul and I touched, I felt an electricity between us, and I wondered if he felt it too. Against my will all the feelings I had tried so hard to suppress came flooding back.

Before I knew it our waltz was over, and I realized that for the first time we had made it through the entire scene without a hitch.

"Bravo! Bravo!" Shawn shouted excitedly, and began to clap. "Now, *that's* what I call a performance!"

I stood there, smiling, expecting wonderful things to happen. Paul had kissed me! I waited for him to apologize, to compliment me, to do anything that would say he really did care for me.

Glancing up at his face, I expected him to be looking adoringly down at me. But he was looking at a point beyond Shawn, and when I followed his gaze, I realized he was looking at Becky. *Becky!* I hadn't even realized she was there.

I swallowed hard. "Paul?"

"Hmmm?" He looked down at me questioningly.

I hesitated. "Did I—did I skate okay?"

"What? Oh, yeah, you were fine. Good concentration." He smiled at me briefly, then skated off, right toward Becky.

I stood there, a mixture of confusion and

112

misery welling up inside me. I had just skated my best ever, and Paul hadn't even seemed·to notice! As for the electricity I'd felt between us, apparently he had felt nothing at all. There he was, rushing to Becky's side without so much as a backward glance at me. When he reached her, she threw her arms around his neck and gave him a big hug.

"Oh, Paul, you guys were fantastic!" she exclaimed.

I was crushed.

Well, I told myself sadly, *at least I still have Trent and Karen.* I knew they cared about me even if Paul didn't.

But when I looked over at the rink's entrance where I expected to see them waiting for me, they were nowhere in sight. I glanced up in the stand where they had been seated earlier, and they were still there. Only they weren't looking in my direction. Their heads were close together in what seemed to be deep conversation. Karen and Trent hadn't noticed me either.

Feeling very sorry for myself, I left the ice, hurried to my locker, and took off my skates. As soon as I had put on my sneakers and my jacket, I raced out of the building.

113

*   *   *

"Lindsey, telephone!" my mother shouted from downstairs about an hour later.

Slowly, I rolled off my bed and trudged into the hall to pick up the extension. I was pretty sure I knew who it was, and I was right.

"Lindsey? Hi, it's me."

"Hi, Karen," I said.

"So—uh—what's up?"

"Not much."

There was a long pause. "Is something wrong?" Karen asked at last. "You sound kind of weird." When I didn't reply, she continued. "Did something happen at rehearsal this afternoon? It looked as if everything was going real well."

"That's not the reason I'm upset," I said sharply. Paul's dropping me like a hot potato to rush over to Becky was bad enough, but my best friend's ignoring me had hurt almost as much—maybe more—and I lost it. "I can't believe you don't know. You, of all people! I'm upset because you didn't even notice the best performance I've ever given in a very difficult part! I'm upset because you were too busy talking to Trent to pay any attention to me at all!"

Karen sighed. "Oh, Lindsey, I was afraid this

114

would happen. We never meant it to. I'm so sorry! It's just that with all the time we've been spending together lately, we've found out how much we have in common. And I've been out with him only once so far. I was going to tell you, honestly. I just didn't know how."

I felt as though I had just entered the twilight zone. "What are you talking about?"

"About Trent and me," Karen said. "Isn't that what you're all bent out of shape about? Believe me, Lindsey, I didn't mean to steal him from you!"

Karen and Trent? Suddenly everything fell into place, and it made me feel even angrier and more betrayed. "Oh, right!" I shouted. "Haven't you just been telling me how you and Trent have *sooo* much in common that you've been sneaking out together behind my back?"

"But, Lindsey . . ."

"I can't believe you'd do that to me, Karen! You're supposed to be my best friend!"

Now Karen was getting angry. "Wait a minute! It's not as though you ever really liked Trent. You were just using him! You never cared about him at all!" she cried. "Trent practically worshipped the ground you walked on, but you never gave him the time of day until you decided to try to make Paul jealous. You said you didn't want to hurt him, but you sure did!"

She took a deep breath and continued before I could get a word in edgewise. "And another thing. Just because you're this—this ice princess all of a sudden doesn't mean that the world revolves around you! All you ever talk about is skating and Paul and the production, and I'm sick and tired of it! I know I said I'd help you and everything, but I need someone to listen to *me* sometimes. You're not the only one with problems, you know!"

Tears streamed down my cheeks. I couldn't defend myself because I knew she was right. I had been incredibly selfish. I *had* used Trent to make Paul jealous, and where had it gotten me? Exactly nowhere. Trent had been hurt, Karen was mad, Paul liked Becky, and none of them wanted to have anything more to do with me.

"Look," Karen went on more quietly. "I apologize for going out with Trent behind your back. It was wrong, and I'm sorry. But you have to admit the way you treated him was pretty crummy. And you know what? The funny thing is that he knew Paul was the one

116

you really liked all along. But Trent was so crazy about you that he figured any attention at all was better than none."

I couldn't think of a thing to say. Things were so messed up that I didn't know of any way I could straighten them out.

When I remained silent, Karen said coolly, "Well, that's about it, I guess. Call me later if you want to talk." With that, she hung up.

Returning to my room, I threw myself down on the bed and sobbed. This was the first major fight I'd ever had with Karen, and it made me feel just awful.

On top of everything else, there was "Snow White." The opening was only a few days away, and the very thought of it made my stomach churn. Not because I wasn't physically prepared—I had proved I was today during rehearsal. But emotionally I'd never be ready. Being around Paul so much and skating with him in our romantic duet only reminded me that it was Becky he cared about, not me. The kiss that had meant so much to me meant nothing to him.

If only the whole thing were already over, I thought miserably. *Then I could avoid Paul and Becky, and I'd never skate again!*

But even as the thought crossed my mind, I knew I could never give up skating. Over the past few weeks my passion for it had returned. Being on the ice gave me a sense of accomplishment and self-worth. I *was* good—Karen had been right. I *did* have talent, but until the ice show, I'd lacked the incentive to keep going. And now it seemed that skating was the only good thing left in my entire life.

How ironic it was that just a month ago I'd thought Paul might be interested in me, and Trent was following me around like a little puppy dog! Now I had lost them both. But losing Karen's friendship was more than I could stand. Blinking back my tears, I ran into the hallway to call her.

I was just picking up the phone when my father called, "Lindsey, Karen's here."

When I raced down, I found her waiting for me at the foot of the stairs. I could tell she'd been crying too.

"Lin," Karen whispered tearfully, "nothing and nobody is worth losing my very best friend. I'm sorry for all those things I said!"

We flung our arms around each other. "Oh, Karen, I'm sorry for the way I acted," I sobbed.

"I probably would have done the same thing if I were in your shoes," Karen admitted. "I may have been too quick to judge. After all, you've been under a lot of pressure."

I shook my head. "It doesn't excuse what I did. You're right—the whole world doesn't revolve around me. I'm sorry I've been so selfish. I could handle losing Trent and even Paul, but without you *I'd* be lost!"

We were both wiping the tears from our cheeks when Luke came in.

"What is this?" he joked good-naturedly. "Are you two rehearsing for a soap opera or something?"

Karen and I looked at each other and started to giggle. I guess it did sort of look that way.

"Hey," Karen said, "why don't we get out of here and go talk for a while? I know the perfect place. . . ."

"The ice cream parlor!" I said, grinning. We were both laughing when we walked out the front door.

Chapter Ten

"Well, what do you think?"

It was opening night of the ice show, and Karen stood behind me as I gazed at my reflection in my bedroom mirror. I was hardly able to believe it was really me. Karen had french-braided my hair, leaving a few wispy tendrils to frame my face. And my costume was absolutely perfect. It was white chiffon with a sweetheart neckline, a beaded bodice, and a soft, full skirt.

"Oh, Karen," I whispered, "thank you! I've never felt so beautiful in my whole life. I don't know what I'd do without you!"

Laughing, she said, "Hey, that's what best

friends are for, right? Now, get your stuff together, Snow White, so we can leave for the
rink. You don't want to keep all those dwarfs
waiting."

We pulled on our heavy jackets and gloves
and hurried downstairs.

"Oh, honey, I love your hair! Let us see your
outfit!" Mom exclaimed as we came into the
kitchen. Luke and Dad were there too.

I was about to unzip my jacket, when Karen
stopped me. "*No!* I mean, don't you want it to
be a surprise?"

Dad smiled. "Okay. I guess we can wait
until the show begins. Break a leg, honey,"
he added, giving me a quick kiss on the
forehead.

"*Dad!*" I wailed.

"Mellow out, sis," Luke chuckled, and
punched me playfully on the arm. "It's just a
show-biz expression. It means good luck."

Mom came up to me and nervously fingered
my bangs. "Now, don't be nervous, dear.
You'll do fine."

"Yeah." Luke grinned mischievously. "And
even if you foul up, I'm taping the whole thing
so we'll be able to watch it over, and over, and
over, and—"

"Luke!" I exclaimed, but I wasn't really angry. How could I be when my whole family was looking at me with so much pride in their eyes? I only hoped I wouldn't let them down.

I waved good-bye and Karen and I got into her car. Neither of us said a word the whole way to the rink—I was too wrapped up in my own thoughts, and Karen understood that.

As I looked out the car window at the houses we passed, I wondered how many of the people inside would be watching "Snow White"—and me—on television, and my stomach lurched.

Then my thoughts turned to Paul, and I sighed wistfully. If only things had turned out differently between us! I wouldn't be so nervous about the show if I knew I had his love and support. But though my heart fluttered wildly every time we skated together, my Prince Charming was only faking it.

"Well, here we are." Karen interrupted my sorrowful thoughts as she pulled up to the front entrance of the rink. "I'll drop you off here, okay?"

I nodded. "Sure. What are you going to do until the show starts?"

Karen avoided my eyes. "Well, actually I'm

going to go pick up Trent. We've got front row tickets, you know."

"Yes, I know," I said. "It's okay, Karen, honestly. I'm glad you two got together. Trent and I were really wrong for each other, but you and he make a great couple. I'm happy for you both!"

Now Karen looked at me and smiled radiantly. "Thanks, Lin. Well, guess you'd better get inside. The star can't be late for her big debut, can she? And remember," she added, "we'll both be right there, cheering you on!"

"Just like you've been all along," I said. Then I picked up my bag and went into the rink.

The dressing rooms were a scene of mass confusion. Kids were running around everywhere, looking for missing costumes and shouting words of encouragement to one another.

Shawn suddenly appeared behind me and tapped me on the shoulder. "Can I talk to you in my office a moment, Lindsey?"

"Sure." I followed him to his office, wondering what he was going to say.

"Close the door, would you?" he asked when we got there. "I swear, those kids are making enough noise to raise the dead!"

"So—uh—what did you want to talk to me about?" I asked nervously.

Smiling, Shawn said, "I just wanted to let you know how proud I am of you."

"But the show hasn't even started yet," I pointed out, puzzled. "I mean, what if I fall or something?"

Shawn shook his head. "How well you actually skate tonight doesn't matter, Lindsey. Because of you, all those kids out there who've worked so hard have a chance to perform." He paused, and then continued. "I realize how tough it's been for you, taking over the role of Snow White on such short notice, and I want you to know how much I appreciate it. Tonight you'll see it's been worth all the hard work and the aggravation. And you are going to be absolutely terrific."

"Thanks," I said softly. "I just wish that Becky hadn't been hurt. She would have done so much better."

Shawn shook his head. "No. *You'll* do better. And you know why?"

I stared at him blankly.

"Because," he said, "you're the better skater."

I was astonished. "But . . ."

"No buts. Becky may have more experience and a more polished technique, but she lacks the very things that make you so breathtaking to watch out on the ice. Aside from grace and style, you have a marvelous spontaneity that makes every move fresh and exciting."

"But—but I thought Becky was perfect," I managed to say.

Shawn smiled. "Nobody's perfect, Lindsey. Becky's technique comes pretty close, I grant you that. But when you skate, you become one with the music. Every move you make tells a story, and that's how it should be."

I was so thrilled by his praise that I was speechless. My head was spinning.

Then Shawn said something that really threw me. "Now, if you and Paul would only get together and settle this lovers' quarrel of yours . . ."

"What?" I squawked, my face turning beet red. "You've got it all wrong, Shawn! He and Becky are going together. Paul doesn't even *like* me!"

Shawn grinned. "Lindsey, when you've been around as long as I have, you recognize the signals. And I'm telling you, that boy has it bad for you."

Much as I would have liked to believe him,

it just didn't make sense. If Paul had it bad for me, why didn't he show it?

Shawn rubbed his chin. "Now, I don't usually meddle in other people's business, but I think you two need to get your feelings out in the open before you go on tonight. If you do, I can just about guarantee you'll both give the performances of your lives."

Just then there was a knock on the door, and when it slowly opened, Becky stuck her head in. "Hi—I'm sorry to bug you guys, but page eighteen of my script is missing. Do you have the master, Shawn?" Since she couldn't skate in the production, Shawn had made Becky the narrator.

"Sure, come on in." Shawn rummaged through a stack of papers on his desk and pulled out a binder. Then, glancing at his watch, he said, "Uh-oh—I've got to run and check on a few things. Becky, find the page you need in here, and then Lindsey can make a copy for you on the machine."

I went rigid. The last thing I wanted was to be alone with Becky!

"You look really gorgeous in that costume, Lindsey," Becky said as the door closed behind Shawn.

"Uh—thanks," I mumbled. Then I burst out with "Becky, I can't tell you how sorry I am—about the accident, I mean. You should be wearing this costume and skating tonight, not me."

Becky smiled at me, her eyes misty. "I won't pretend that I'm not upset about not being able to perform. I am. But the accident wasn't your fault, Lindsey. *I'm* the one who ran into *you*, remember?" She shrugged. "It was just one of those freak things. Besides, there'll be other productions."

She began leafing through the notebook, searching for the page she needed. Without looking up she added, "But, you know, I *am* kind of jealous about something else."

"What—what do you mean?" I stammered.

Becky turned toward me. "Paul's in love with you, Lindsey. He has been for a long time."

"He—has?" I could hardly believe my ears. She nodded.

"But I thought you and he—I mean, you're always together, and I thought . . ."

"We're just friends," Becky said a little sadly. "Oh, I admit I was hoping for more than that—what girl wouldn't? But all Paul

127

ever talked about was you, and pretty soon I got the message."

I was in total shock. "But he acts as if I don't even exist!" I exclaimed.

Becky leaned on her crutches and sighed. "He was really hurt when you started dating that other guy. I guess that was just his way of dealing with it."

I groaned. "The only reason I went out with Trent was that I thought Paul liked *you*! And then after the accident, things just got worse and worse."

"I know," Becky said. "I tried to get him to talk to you about it, but he wouldn't listen. Paul's awfully stubborn. Maybe you should talk to him tonight before you skate."

"That's what Shawn said," I admitted, "but I don't think I can! Besides, what makes you think he'll listen?"

"Maybe he won't. Then again, he just might. It's worth a try, isn't it?"

I looked down at the floor and then at Becky again. "Why? I mean, why do you want us to patch things up?"

She smiled. "Because Paul's a great guy. He deserves someone special, and since it's not going to be me, then it ought to be you. Lately

Paul's become one of my best friends. But he's miserable, and I hate to see him like that. I think you could fix it."

"I don't know, Becky," I murmured. "It's so hard for me to open up to a guy about my feelings, especially Paul."

"Just promise me you'll try." She pulled the paper she needed out of the binder and began to hobble out the door.

"Don't you want me to copy it for you?" I called after her.

"Oh, no," Becky said, "I'll be okay. You'd better go find Paul."

I stared after her as she left. Was what she said really true? Would Paul listen if I explained to him, or was it too late?

Back in the dressing room Shawn had just finished giving everyone a quick pep talk as I entered.

"Okay, group, this is it!" he announced. "This is what we've all been working for. Go out there and make me proud. But most of all—have fun!"

Everybody cheered.

"The show starts in ten minutes," he went on. "We've got a full house out there, and we don't want to keep them waiting!"

Ten minutes? I glanced in horror at the clock, then found my bag, took out my skates, and laced them on with shaking fingers.

"Hey, are you okay, Lindsey?" a girl to my right asked softly. "You look awfully pale."

"Yeah, I'm okay," I assured her. "Just a little nervous, that's all."

I hurried out of the room and began frantically looking around for Paul. Where was he? I didn't see him anywhere. How could I clear the air between us if I couldn't even find him?

"Places, please," Shawn called out, and we all scurried to take our positions for the first scene.

Then I heard Becky's voice over the loudspeaker, beginning the narration of "Snow White." Shawn gave us our cue and the wicked queen and I sailed out onto the ice, bright spotlights following our every move.

I willed myself to forget everything else and concentrate on my skating with every ounce of energy I had. It worked—my nervousness evaporated. I was able to block out all the people sitting in the stands and even the TV cameras as I thought only about my role.

Almost before I knew it, the scene was over

130

and we skated off, passing the dwarfs, whose first brief scene was about to begin.

And suddenly I saw him.

"Paul!" I exclaimed. He looked so handsome in a red and black belted tunic over black tights and wearing a small golden crown on his head that I caught my breath.

Paul nodded abstractedly in my direction, then turned his attention back to the rink, glancing down at the notes on his clipboard. He might have been dressed as Prince Charming, but I knew that until the final scene, his main responsibility was to act as Shawn's assistant. I also knew that this was probably the worst time to initiate a conversation, but I couldn't help myself.

Coming over to his side, I whispered, "Paul, can we talk?"

He frowned. "Now? Have you got a problem?"

"Well, yes, kind of. Not a skating problem," I assured him quickly. "It's personal. I talked to Becky tonight—and Shawn said—I mean, I just wanted to tell you . . ."

I realized I was babbling, so I tried again.

"Paul, what I want to say . . ."

Suddenly the music changed and I recognized my cue.

"You're on," Paul said matter-of-factly.

I took a deep breath and swept back onto the ice. This was my first solo, and the spotlight was focused on me alone. Once again I made a major effort to immerse myself in the role of Snow White. Remembering what Shawn had said about my movements telling a story, I let my body flow with the music.

"Good job, Lindsey," Paul said when I finished. At least, that's what I think he said—I could hardly hear him over the applause.

"Thanks," I gasped, breathless from the exertions of my solo.

As the wicked queen and the huntsman made their entrance, followed by several trees and forest animals, Paul looked at me instead of at his clipboard for a change. "So what did you want to tell me?" he asked.

I swallowed hard. This was my chance. If only I didn't blow it! "I—I just wanted to say—I want you to know that—well, that I like you. A lot," I blurted out.

After what Becky and Shawn had told me, I'd hoped Paul would be delighted by this piece of news. Instead, he just stared at me. "You sure have a funny way of showing it!"

"Well, what was I supposed to do?" I exclaimed. "Ever since the accident you've been acting like I don't exist. I don't blame you for being mad at me for it, but even before it happened you said you couldn't go to the Winter Formal with me because you had to work on the production. So when I saw you with Becky that night at Rose's Cafe, I thought you two were dating, and . . ."

Shaking his head, Paul said, "You sure do jump to conclusions, don't you? I *was* working, but Becky had a private lesson with Shawn that night and when it was over, we went out to get something to eat. Friends do that sometimes, you know. And Becky and I are friends."

"That's what she told me tonight," I mumbled. "And she also said—"

Paul cut me off angrily. "Besides, why should you care if we were dating or not? Isn't one boyfriend enough for you?"

"Trent's not my boyfriend," I cried. "He never was!"

Before Paul could respond, the wicked queen exited. That meant it was time for my next entrance, and I glided into the center of the rink. In this dramatic scene the huntsman tries to carry out the queen's orders to kill Snow White but can't bring himself to do it. I guess my distress at the way my conversation with Paul was going must have added realism to my performance, because the audience applauded like mad as the scene ended.

The minute I came off the ice, avoiding the dwarfs who were rushing on, I said to Paul, "The only reason I went out with Trent was to make you jealous!"

His eyes widened. "Really?"

I hung my head. "I know it was rotten to use Trent like that—he's an awfully nice guy. But I guess that's what love does to a person."

I hadn't meant to say that last sentence. It just kind of popped out, and as soon as it did, I could feel myself turning scarlet with embarrassment. I wanted to run away and hide, but of course I couldn't.

"Did you say *love*?" Paul asked softly.

I nodded, unable to look at him.

"Lindsey . . ." Paul reached out and cupped my chin in his hand, raising my head so I was forced to meet his eyes. "I guess I've been pretty stupid."

"No, you haven't," I replied miserably. "You thought only what I meant you to think— about Trent and me, I mean. And as I said before, I don't blame you for being mad at me about the accident—"

"I admit I was kind of upset, but the only person I was mad at was me," Paul interrupted. "I never should have let Becky talk me into letting her drive my sister's precious car. The whole thing was my fault, not yours or hers. And now there's something I want to tell you—"

"Lindsey!" Shawn snapped frantically from behind us. "Wake up! You're on!"

Realizing that I had almost missed my cue, I sped out for my first scene with the seven dwarfs. I would be on the ice from then until the end of the show, so I wouldn't have another chance to talk to Paul before our scene together.

As I cavorted with the dwarfs and the forest animals, I was glad that I had learned my part so thoroughly. While I was going through the motions, all I could think about was Paul. How did he really feel about me? What if Shawn and Becky were wrong, and he didn't care for me at all?

The wicked queen, now disguised as a feeble old woman, appeared, and the dwarfs went marching off to the mine. As we skated together while she offered me the shiny red apple, I was thinking, *Paul doesn't blame me for the accident, thank goodness, and he's not in love with Becky. But that doesn't mean he's in love with me.* What had he been about to tell me a moment ago? I wondered. Would I ever find out?

At last I accepted the apple and bit into it, then clutched dramatically at my throat, falling gracefully at the witch's feet. The dwarfs returned and skated in sad circles around me, mourning their beloved Snow White. The scene ended with a blackout, during which the golden casket slid into place and I lay down on top of it.

Then the lights came up again. I waited, motionless, hardly daring to breathe. This was it, the final scene when the prince awakens Snow White with a kiss. Would Paul fake it the way he had during rehearsals every time but once?

I heard Prince Charming's music and the whoosh of blades cutting into the ice, followed by a round of enthusiastic applause as Paul made his entrance. I couldn't watch his sorrowful solo, since I had to keep my eyes closed, but I'd seen it in rehearsals so often that I could easily visualize Paul's power and grace.

Soon I heard him coming nearer and nearer. My heart began to pound wildly as Paul stopped beside the casket and took my hand in his. Opening one eye the tiniest bit, I saw him bend over until his face was so close to mine that I could feel his warm breath on my cheek. It was almost like slow motion, or like a dream.

But then his lips, warm and gentle, pressed mine, and I knew it wasn't a dream. Paul was kissing me as if he really meant it and not as if he were just following stage directions. When the kiss ended and I opened my eyes, gazing directly into his, all my questions were answered.

Smiling, Paul helped me to my feet and we began to waltz around the ice in each other's arms. My body seemed to melt against his as we dipped and swirled, and when he lifted me effortlessly, I felt like a bird floating in a sun-filled sky.

The music rose to a crescendo, and as our dance ended, the audience was silent for a brief moment. Then suddenly they were on their feet, clapping, whistling, and cheering.

Holding hands, Paul and I bowed to the audience and then to each other, smiling into each other's eyes.

"You did it, Lindsey!" he shouted over the din. As the rest of the cast came out to take their bows, he said something else I couldn't hear.

"What?" I shouted back.

"I said, *I love you!*" Paul yelled. Then, right in front of everybody, he pulled me close and kissed me again. And the fact that this kiss wasn't in the script made it even sweeter!